THE PUR

When Dr Michael Lloyd comes to St Jude's, more than one nurse is intrigued. But is Staff Nurse Elizabeth Fletcher being really honest when she says she is more interested in him as a doctor than as a romantic possibility?

THE PURSUIT OF DR LLOYD

BY

MARJORIE NORRELL

MILLS & BOON LIMITED
London · Sydney · Toronto

First published in Great Britain 1970
by Mills & Boon Limited, 15–16 Brook's Mews,
London W1A 1DR

This edition 1982

© Mills & Boon 1970

Australian copyright 1982
Philippine copyright 1982

ISBN 0 263 73972 4

03/0882

Set in 10 on 12 pt Linotron Times

Photoset by Rowland Phototypesetting Ltd
Bury St Edmunds, Suffolk
Made and printed in Great Britain by
Richard Clay (The Chaucer Press) Ltd
Bungay, Suffolk

CHAPTER ONE

'Pop some more bread in the toaster, will you, Joan?' Elizabeth pressed the tip of her pencil to her lip and frowned. She was making out the shopping list to leave at the corner shop on her way to St Jude's, the General Hospital where she and Joan Barstow, her flat-mate, were both staff nurses. 'Will we really need more of that rye bread stuff of yours this week?' she asked consideringly.

'It's since I've been getting the cheesy flavoured sort,' Joan said apologetically. 'You don't know what a temptation it is to eat twice as much every time!'

'I still maintain you'd be far better off to stick to a sensible ordinary diet,' Elizabeth opined, adding not unkindly, 'and stop eating so much sugar and sweets and chocolates! That's where you add the ounces, *not* in your daily food intake! Why don't you give it a trial, just for a month, say? I'm certain if you cut down your sugar intake by half, ate an apple or an orange when you sit reading or viewing, and didn't patronise the walk-around girl when you go to the pictures, you'd soon be my weight at least!'

'And I'd be thoroughly miserable for the rest of my days!' Joan laughed, and deftly slid two more slices of bread into the toaster. 'No, thank you very much! Half the pleasure in my trips to the cinema lies in the sticky choc-ice bars, and the little box of sugared almonds on my knee. As for eating apples and oranges when I'm viewing—! That would be the end! Imagine sucking an orange just when the murderer was about to be discovered! Takes the edge off things, somehow!'

'Try watching travel films, then,' Elizabeth laughed, and applied marmalade to her toast with brisk, sure movements. 'When you've finished eating your pressed-out straw,' she gave one brief glance at the slimming wafer Joan was spreading thinly with peanut butter, 'we'd better get a move on. Today's the first day for the new doctor, isn't it? We'd better be on our toes until we find out what he's like.'

'I know what he's like.' Joan crunched the remains of her crispbread with firm white teeth. 'He's tall and fair and worried-looking, and he doesn't look in any way like a consultant physician! He looks more like a musician who isn't quite certain of where he's going, a sort of lost-little-boy-worried-to-death look, if you know what I mean?'

'Not exactly.' Elizabeth rose from the table and began to stack the pots neatly on to a tray which she carried over to the corner of the small flat where a cupboard-like arrangement did duty as a kitchen. 'Sister Murdoch did say there'd been some sort of family tragedy in his life a year or so ago. Something to do with his brother, I think she said, who was working overseas somewhere. I don't know the details, but whatever they are they may well account for the look of tragedy. Unless,' she added mischievously, 'that's another of your romantic flights of fancy, love!'

'It's not!' Joan was emphatic on this point, but not upset. She was well used to the other's teasing references to her own ability to lose herself completely in any drama, either of stage, screen or the printed word, providing there was an equal element of tragedy and romance involved. 'Maybe he's been jilted or something,' she offered. 'No one seems to know whether or not he's married, though Mary Walker did say she'd heard he'd been looking for a flat as near to the hospital as possible.'

'She'd better tell him number five's to be vacant next week, then, or hadn't you heard?' Elizabeth was almost ready to leave. 'Do get a move on, Joan! If we walk briskly we can get there in ample time and needn't wait for the bus!'

'I'm not as energetic as you are, not first thing in the morning,' Joan grumbled good-naturedly as she pulled on her own coat, adding an indifferent reminder to Elizabeth that 'drying the dishes could wait till we get home. They won't get germs in here! They wouldn't dare, not the way you scour the place all the time. Why you insist on this morning walk on these chilly mornings I'll never know,' she continued as Elizabeth dropped the latch and tried the door carefully. 'It may be good for the figure, but I'm always hungry again when we get to the hospital! What I've walked off I put right back on in the self-service canteen!'

'Then get a glass of milk and some fruit,' Elizabeth advised. 'Keep off the sweetened tea and biscuits! You'd soon find a tremendous difference, and one which would please you!'

'I'll try it,' Joan offered unexpectedly. 'It's Lent this week, I know 'cos Gran wrote and reminded me. When I was a kiddie I used to give up sweets. When I was a teenager I tried keeping my temper for the whole of Lent. That wasn't too difficult,' she grinned. 'Gran used to say it was too easy, because I was too easy-going to lose my temper in the first place, and maybe she was right! This year I'll try your slimming advice and, although I know I can't give it up, I really will cut down on all sweets—including sugar—and eat fruit instead of ices and chocolates! I'll be doing myself a really good turn—if it works—and indulging in what Gran calls "some decent self-discipline" at one and the same time. How's that?'

'It can't do any harm, and may well do a power of good,' Elizabeth smiled. 'Hurry now, or we'll be late after all!'

Obediently Joan hurried, but her extra weight and the fact that she could never keep silent for long together made it extra difficult for her to keep pace with her friend.

'Did you say number five was to be let, Liz?' she panted. 'That means the Frazers must have got their sailing date?'

'They have. They're on their way to Canada early next week and they're spending their last few days in England with her mother and father, a last-minute endeavour to persuade them to decide to follow, I believe. Why?'

''Cos I'll tell Mary,' Joan decided. 'She's always just finishing on my ward when I get in.' Mary had been a ward maid at St Jude's long before either of the girls had gone there, and considered herself a definite part of the establishment. 'She'll let the doctor know,' Joan concluded.

'And let you know why he wants a flat when he's got a room in Jude's as well, eh?' Elizabeth smiled. 'He must have a sound enough reason. Maybe he wants to do further work and needs somewhere quiet and private. Maybe he just wants to "get away from it all" when he's off duty? Anyway,' they parted at the entrance to the day staff cloakroom, 'that's his affair, though I've no doubt whatsoever that Mary and yourself will make it your business as well!'

'No man is an island, didn't someone say once?' Joan retorted, then, laughing as she saw Elizabeth's look of astonishment at the mere idea of Joan using a quotation, she went off to leave her outdoor things and change into the clean uniform which was always awaiting her.

It was funny, Elizabeth reflected as she made the necessary change and eyed herself in the small mirror above the washbasins, how greatly the friendship between herself and Joan had developed. When they had first met in PTS she remembered not being very keen on the jolly-looking girl who seemed to be always munching. Gradually, Joan's unfailing good humour, her absorption in the affairs of those of whom she had grown fond and for whom she would do her level best—providing they gave her all details of whatever concerns absorbed them—had evoked in the more elegant and restrained Elizabeth a genuine and very real affection. When she was given permission to take a flat and live out of the Nurses' Home providing she could find a friend willing to share the place with her, she had turned to Joan Barstow, who had been made a staff nurse at the same time as Elizabeth herself.

On the whole the arrangement worked very well, although in many ways the two girls were entirely the opposite of one another. Elizabeth loved her work and was determined to continue from staff nurse to Ward Sister to, with a little more work and, she thought wryly, a great deal more luck, eventually Deputy Matron somewhere. It would be impossible to imagine herself ever attaining such a position at St Jude's, but there were thousands of other hospitals and she felt convinced that if she worked hard enough and tried hard enough she would eventually achieve her goal.

Joan's ambitions were of an entirely different character. She was an excellent nurse, but she did not see herself spending the rest of her life dedicated to the cause of duty. She made no secret of the fact that what she really wanted in the long run was a home of her own, an adoring husband, preferably someone in the medical world, and a swarm of the children she adored.

'And she'll always have a houseful of pets, a string of dependent relations and no end of chores from sitting on endless committees for everything under the sun,' Elizabeth reflected, smiling at the mental picture this presented.

A glance at her watch informed her that it was high time she was presenting herself on the Ward. Sister Murdoch was a small, tight figure of a woman, but her size gave absolutely no idea of her outstanding capacity for sheer hard work, a capacity she expected from her nurses in an equal degree.

Sister on Casualty ward for some time now, she had developed what she always spoke of as 'a hard shell', but her nurses and the rest of the staff of St Jude's knew this was merely a cloak for a heart as big as it was possible for a heart to be.

Elizabeth was in the ward a full minute before Sister put in her appearance, a fact which she realised Sister had noted and was pleased about. She liked her nurses to be ahead of change-over time, for Jude's was a busy hospital on the outskirts of Malenchester, and close to the motorway which, ironical although it always seemed to Elizabeth, accounted for any number of their patients who, having injured themselves being in too much of a hurry to reach their destination, had to spend up to months sometimes lying in bed and, presumably, reflecting what they had intended to do with the time they had hoped to save.

Dutifully she accompanied Sister to listen to the Night Sister's report. There had been three admissions, one but a few hours ago who was still down in theatre.

'X-ray showed a broken shoulder and wrist and a compound fracture of the right leg. Attempted suicide. He jumped from Hepburns' shop roof and the police brought him in. There's a policeman waiting to see him, Sister,' ran the report. 'Seems he was in some sort of trouble.'

'Well,' Sister Murdoch compressed her lips firmly, 'if he wasn't then he is now, don't you think? What else?'

There had been a motor-cycle accident with the girl pillion passenger now comfortably ensconced in the women's surgical ward. Her fiancé had been fortunate, but was waiting, distraught, in the waiting room.

'I'll see him in a minute,' Ann Murdoch announced.

'Two abdominal emergencies,' came the further report, 'and they're both in Mr Astair's beds in ward five. Apart from that it's been fairly quiet.'

Night Sister and her staff prepared to depart when there was a sound of an ambulance outside the door.

'Mornin', Sister Murdoch,' the driver grinned at her as the two nurses came forward for the stretcher. 'My third trip here tonight. Can't say but that I'll not be relieved to get off duty, just as soon as we've unloaded. This is for White Rose, really, but I knew we'd never make it in time. I'll be surprised if we've made it as it is.'

Accustomed to the man's garrulity, Sister moved forward to see for herself and to take charge.

'Breech birth,' she announced crisply. 'Get her into the small side ward in Women's Medical until someone can arrange for Mr Anstruther to take a look at her.'

After that there was no time to wonder about the new Junior Consultant Physician and his worries, whatever they might be, about living accommodation. Casualty was always busy, and today it seemed to Elizabeth that there would never be an end to the stream of cuts, burns, falls and, in one instance, a pneumonia which, as Sister declared, ought to have been spotted hours ago.

She was tired in mind and body when she crossed to the self-service canteen for a welcome cup of coffee before going home. Lately Elizabeth had walked to and from the hospital. She liked the freshness of the spring mornings, and she loved the feeling of the wind on her hair after hours on the ward. Tonight, for some reason, she knew she could not walk the short distance home to the block of flats—really a huge house conveniently divided by its owners in small, self-contained flatlets— and the detour involved in the collection of the groceries ordered that morning at the corner shop.

'I'll get the bus,' she decided. 'It goes round by the shops and if I pick up the groceries I've only a little way to carry them. I can cut through the passageway . . .'

'Excuse me.' She looked up in surprise as the tall, lean young man in the white coat looked down on her. 'I'm Dr Lloyd,' he began in explanation. 'I think—I hope— you are Staff Nurse Fletcher?'

'You're quite right.' Elizabeth's natural courtesy had diagnosed his shyness. 'Can I help you?'

'I'm told you might,' he said cautiously, 'and I most

sincerely hope my information is correct. Staff Nurse Barstow—I think she said that was her name, she's on Children's—said you knew someone who might have a flat vacant shortly. Is that correct?'

Elizabeth smiled inwardly. Just like Joan, she decided, to be the first of the pair to meet the man and then put the onus of telling him about number five on her flatmate! She felt certain she could guess why Joan had acted this way! She was more than conscious of her slightly plump figure, and the fact that her uniform emphasised it rather than offered the opportunity to disguise the extra inches as did the specially slimming garments she wore on her off-duty days! Joan, she knew, would hope to make a better impression when she met the new doctor in her home surroundings, as it were.

'That's more or less correct,' she said quietly. 'The flat's in the block where we—Nurse Barstow and myself—have a flat, though they're really glorified flatlets, but sufficient, if you know what I mean. I suppose,' she qualified so that he would not be too curious as to why Joan couldn't have told him herself, 'she realises that as I was the one to take out our lease I know Mr Simmonds a little better than she does, and that might help.'

'Then there really is a chance of a flat almost at once?' he seemed to pounce on the few words which obviously were of the most importance where he was concerned.

'Number five will be to let from Monday—or maybe Saturday evening, if it's not been spoken for already,' Elizabeth told him, and hastily added the necessary explanation.

'Then,' he began almost confidently, then added in an apologetic tone almost at once, 'that is . . . would it be

asking too much of you to beg you to try and see this . . .
Mr Simmonds as soon as possible, please, or to tell me
where I may find him, mentioning your name?'

'I shall see him this evening,' Elizabeth made up her
mind on the instant. 'He lives in the basement, and he
arranges the milk, paper and bread deliveries for us all,
especially those of us who have a change of working
hours from time to time. I,' she coloured slightly, because until this moment she had not been certain how
she felt about Matron's suggestion that morning of a
proposed change-over for herself, but all at once she
knew she wanted to do this. Sister Worthington was to
be Senior Sister for Women's Block from Monday, and
Staff Fletcher had been offered the Ward Sistership of
Women's Medical. She was to hand in her affirmation to
Matron in the morning. For a long time she had loved
Casualty and hoped to stay there indefinitely. The con-
stant change of patients had been the greatest attraction.
Now, and without knowing why, she realised she wanted
the Change, and she would write in her affirmation the
moment she reached home.

'I shall be back on the wards from Monday,' she
continued, quite unaware that her long pause had made
him stare at her curiously. 'I'm sorry to sound so vague,
Doctor,' she apologised with her charming smile, 'but
I've been on Casualty for so long I've almost forgotten
any other routine!'

'I shouldn't worry,' he advised, and she saw with
unexpected pleasure how his grey eyes suddenly lit with
pleasurable anticipation. The look was gone in an instant, and, feeling slightly foolish, Elizabeth knew
abruptly that it had nothing to do with her personally.

'You won't forget about the flat, though, will you?' he

said insistently. 'It really is important to me to find somewhere immediately, even if I have to resort to the expense of a room in some hotel.'

'I shall not forget,' Elizabeth assured him quietly. 'If you'd like to call in about half past seven tonight I can take you down to the basement flat to meet Mr Simmonds yourself. You can take it from there, once I've introduced you, can't you?'

'I . . . yes, I should think so.' He seemed abruptly confused, apologetic, and Elizabeth was reminded of Joan's words 'like a little-boy-lost'. He certainly had that look right at this moment, but she mentally shrugged her shoulders and straightened up briskly. .

'Seven-thirty, then, Dr Lloyd,' she announced, confirming her words. 'Here's the address.' She took out her pad and wrote rapidly, tearing off the slip and handing it to him. His long, fine fingers took the slip of paper and folded it carefully, putting it away in his wallet as though it were indeed something of value.

'Thank you, Nurse,' he said politely. 'I'm most grateful,' and before she could think of anything else to say he had turned and was striding rapidly out of sight.

Elizabeth walked home after all. Somehow her tiredness had vanished, and all at once she was looking forward to going back on the wards with her round of days and nights alternating as they used to do.

She collected the small order from the general store and let herself into the flat. Joan should have a meal she would enjoy, but Elizabeth would make certain there was nothing in the menu which would add either an inch or an ounce to her friend's figure.

Elizabeth loved cooking, and hummed gaily to herself as she pottered around the tiny cooking area, her mind busy all the while thinking of the coming summer and her own plans to try, this year, to go to somewhere she had never been. .

'Norway, I think,' she said aloud, just as Joan, puffing after walking upstairs as the lift was—once again—out of order.

'What about Norway?' she demanded, collapsing in a chair and announcing that she had gone through a most exhausting day at one and the same time.

'For my vacation, I think,' Elizabeth turned the flame of the gas higher and warned that the omelettes would be ready in two minutes flat.

'Too cold, I should imagine,' Joan grumbled pleasantly as she went to wash her hands and slip into an off-duty dress. 'And all those trolls and things . . .'

'Silly,' Elizabeth chided. 'You're thinking of the fairy lore! Hasn't all your nursing experience taught you there are no such things?'

'There are . . . inexplicable things,' Joan was surprisingly serious. 'I've learned that! And if it isn't fate, or a Divine Being—and most of what I mean is too trivial for Someone like that—then there *must* be trolls, fairies, or what-have-you! Otherwise how explain the inexplicable, or don't you ever think about it?'

'Often,' Elizabeth acknowledged, placing the fluffy omelette before her friend and turning her attention to her own which was now cooking. 'I'm still fairly child-like, I think, in that way. Maybe because Gran brought me up, but I'm afraid I always put the good things down to a Divine Being, as you say, and the others to His opposite number, as it were. It makes life so much more simple.'

'But life isn't simple,' Joan protested. 'I know it ought

to be, but it isn't. Take that nice Dr Lloyd, for instance. I don't know what's happened to him, but there's tragedy in every line of his face, and he's such a pleasant man. Wait till you meet him!'

'I've met him.' Elizabeth slid her own omelette on to her plate and sat down, eyeing the golden egg and mushroom concoction with some satisfaction. 'He's coming here around seven-thirty. I've promised to take to meet Mr Simmonds.'

'*Here?*' Joan yelped. 'Tonight? Why didn't you tell me? You get in touch with old Simmonds as soon as you've eaten. I'll tidy up round here then you can ask him—the doctor, I mean, not Mr Simmonds—back for coffee . . . We can chat . . .'

Elizabeth smiled and ate her meal unhurriedly, but she knew that by the time she had been down to the caretaker's flat in the basement the small flat would be tidy and spotless.

'Bless her,' she thought warmly of Joan as she ran lightly downstairs to the basement. 'She deserves someone . . . especially nice! Someone who'll take care of her by way of a change!' then she dismissed all worries about Joan from her mind as the deep voice of the caretaker bade her 'come in'.

Elizabeth never minded going down to visit Mr Simmonds in his basement. It would be—for it always was—difficult to get away again, but she knew her visits did the man good, and that it was a relief to him to 'discuss, not talk', as he phrased it, as an antidote to the unending chatter of his wife, Hilda.

Bill was normally a morose individual, except with those few persons he termed 'sympathetic-like' towards him. Elizabeth was the prime one of these favoured few, and as she ran down the stairs to his door she remembered her first visit.

It had been on what she now knew Bill always referred to as 'one o' them days'. These, it transpired, were the days when the memories of his years in the last war, first as a despatch rider and then as an ambulance driver, overwhelmed him. It appeared he had been one of the first people to enter a liberated concentration camp, and the sights he had seen, the stench which had assailed his nostrils, seemed even now to rush over him in all-engulfing tide of misery and horror.

With his permission and before explaining properly the reason for her visit, Elizabeth had made a pot of hot, strong tea which she shared with him. She had listened quietly as he described the nightmares which had periodically affected him since demobilisation. The remembered shock, the pain of the heart and spirit and therefore, more difficult to dismiss than that of a merely physical quality which would pass with the help of medical attention, were acute, she had realised. He had been more filled with grief than with fury, as he realised how long some of the helpless women and men, and even children, had been compelled to endure what he saw as a complete stranger to whom these things had been quite unknown.

After a second spell in a military hospital—the first had been because of a wound and had been considered a cure—was for a nervous breakdown, and although he had returned to service until the time for his demobilisation none of this had, apparently, helped very much. The return to his over-talkative wife Hilda had been only a partial success. Hilda, he had confided, told him, 'Use your loaf and forget all about it. You've done your bit, an' it's no concern of yours or mine, not any more. The thing to do is to forget all that.'

'As if,' Elizabeth had heard the bitterness in his voice as he concluded, 'I'm *trying* to remember! I *want* to forget, heaven knows that! But I just can't, Nurse, an' that's all there is to it!'

Elizabeth had stayed far longer than she had intended on that first visit, but, she felt now, it had been well worth while. She had her RMN as well as her SRN and midwifery, and she had talked to Bill until, almost without his being aware of how it had happened, she had persuaded him to make an appointment to see Mr Paul Ambrose, the junior consultant in psychiatry at St Jude's.

Bill's treatment had taken a matter of two years, and he had consented to be in the psychiatric wing of the hospital for three months, continuing as an outpatient the remainder of the time. Now he was as well and as happy as he could hope to be, she supposed, and certainly the bouts of morbid brooding were becoming more and more rare. Apparently he had never forgotten that it had been Elizabeth who had first tried—and succeeded—to help him, and his gratitude knew no bounds.

He greeted her with a smile and invited her into the snug, over-furnished two rooms and a kitchen with a bathroom attached that he and Hilda called home.

'I'll put the kettle on, Nurse,' he began. 'Won't take a minute. Now,' he remarked with an affable cheerfulness she found a refreshing change since those earlier visits of hers, 'what can I do for you? Plugs, light switches, gas fittings? You name it and leave it to me to fix it. OK?'

'OK, indeed, if it happened to be anything like that,

Bill,' Elizabeth smiled, 'but we're fine. It's just that I heard that the Frazers are going this weekend, and there's a new junior consultant at the hospital seems desperate to find a flat of his own. Don't blame him, especially if he's wanting to do further work, which I understand he is going to do. I wondered . . .'

'He's a friend of yours, is he, Nurse?' Bill's mild blue eyes looked searchingly into her own. 'If he is then that's OK. He can jump the queue and no one but you an' me'll be any the wiser.'

'I can't exactly call him my friend, Bill.' Elizabeth could never be less than completely honest, even when to deceive a little was obviously an advantage. 'I only met him today . . . he only arrived at Jude's this morning, you see, but . . .'

'I think it can be done, Nurse!' Bill poured the tea, two thick cups of it, hot, strong and too well sweetened for Elizabeth's liking, but she swallowed it without protest, realising that to remind Bill she only liked very little sugar in things would upset him. Since his treatment he had prided himself on remembering most of the things he so often forgot, and to let him feel a failure was one sure way to create a setback in his condition, so she drank the tea and kept silent about its flavour.

'Time we had somebody round here you might take a fancy to, Nurse, if you don't mind my speaking out plain-like. Your friend, now, Nurse Barstow, she's not backward at coming forward, as the saying goes though unless a chap likes bit of an armful I'd say she'd lose out every time, if you'd only be a bit more friendly-like with the ones you might fancy yourself!' He gave her a broad wink, which made Elizabeth smile, but she rose to leave. When Bill got on the subject of 'it's time you married and settled down to a home of your own, Nurse,' she always felt it was high time to leave.

'I don't know anything about Dr Lloyd, Bill,' she reminded him cautiously. 'I don't even know whether or not he's already married, but,' her honesty compelled her to add, 'he doesn't *look* married, if you know what I mean? He looks somewhat bewildered and as though no one cares about him very much; I heard there'd been some sort of a personal tragedy in his life lately. That may have something to do with it, I'm afraid I just don't know, but I promised to try and help if I could.'

'Well,' Bill opened the door with a flourish, 'you have, if that's any comfort. Tell him to pop down and see me. If I think he's good enough for the best nurse in Malenchester, the flat's his.'

'Thanks, Bill.' Elizabeth shook hands because she knew it pleased him. 'I told him to call round at my place around half-seven, so when he comes I'll send him down to you. All right?'

'Fine,' Bill agreed cheerfully. 'An' I shall warn him that if he does anything to upset you in any way I'll find some method of getting him out as fast as he got in, whether he's signed an agreement or not!'

'I don't think there'll be anything like that to worry about, Bill!' Elizabeth said lightly, then, to change the subject and to make her escape, since this was something about which Bill refused to talk very much, 'how is Hilda's rheumatism these days?'

'Good enough, when she wants to go playing Bingo!' he said with some disgust. 'That's where she is tonight, as I expect you've guessed. A fried supper is what I'll get even though she knows they don't agree with my inside any more! No consideration, that's what it is. But I expect I can find something to tide me over if I look round the larder.'

'I've a tin of ready-to-serve rice pudding in the cupboard,' Elizabeth offered. 'If you like I'll send it down with Dr Lloyd when he calls. Won't take a jiffy to heat up, and you can put fruit with it, you know. Would you like a bottle of those pears I did last autumn? We've a few left.'

'Thanks, Nurse,' Bill nodded appreciatively in anticipation. 'If Hilda'd think like that we'd save money, but it's all easy ways where she's concerned. Says she had enough of makin' do when I was in the Forces and in the rationing after. That's what *she* ought to forget!' he added with a wry chuckle.

'Looking back never does anyone much good,' Elizabeth said, smiling. 'I'll send them down, and I'd advise you to warm the pears, just slightly.'

'I'll remember,' Bill agreed. 'Thanks, Nurse. Your friend's as good as installed if he's anything like at all, which he must be or you'd never have spoken up for him this way!'

Elizabeth made no comment, merely waving gaily and starting out back upstairs. She knew nothing at all of Dr Lloyd, she reminded herself. There had been nothing save that brief meeting just before she left Jude's. That and the gossip as repeated by Joan earlier—*and* later, she reflected—and altogether it didn't amount to much.

'He looked a decent sort of person,' she frowned, concentrating. 'In fact, if he were going into general practice I'd say he's just the sort of man to inspire confidence in all his patients, right from the start, and to gain more as he goes on! Apart from that . . .'

Abruptly she made herself stop thinking about the

somewhat forlorn-looking young man she had encountered earlier that day. As Joan had said, there was *something* very appealing, in the way he looked so competent at his job and, paradoxically, so incapable of dealing with the everyday matters of the world and living.

'It's none of my affair, anyhow,' she reminded herself as she reached her own door. 'I've done what I said I'd do. Now, when he calls—*if* he calls—I'll tell him how to reach Mr Simmonds, and it'll be up to him from there onwards!'

Elizabeth sighed as she opened the door. She had hoped for a quiet evening reading the new book she had brought from the library only the previous weekend, but now there would be the flat to put into apple-pie order, because she hated untidiness 'beyond all reason', as Joan often said.

'When my friends come to visit me,' was Joan's dictum, 'I take it for granted it's the pleasure of my company they're seeking, not a room without a speck of dust, a faded flower or everything just precisely where it should be! I can play housewife with anyone, when if comes to a point, but I'd never make a fetish of the place as you do! If you ever get married—and it's no use shaking your head, because it may well happen one day—you'll drive even the most understanding man round the bend if you don't relax a bit now and again. Ashtrays are there to be filled! Coffee stains on the tiles aren't a major catastrophe, and not even on the carpet now there are so many fine cleaning things around! You'd have done fine in the "good old days", when every housewife even made her own soap and candles! Give me the present day with its drip-drys, instant foods, stain-removers, permanent polishes, the lot! I'd never want to make a martyr of myself like the good wives of the "covered wagon" days!'

Consequently it came as a surprise, almost a shock, when Elizabeth opened the door and went into the flat. The room had been reasonably tidy when she had left it. Now everything that could shine really shone so that it was possible to see one's face in the small table, now cleared of the brief meal and the tablecloth out of sight. The crockery, Elizabeth noted automatically, had been washed, dried and stacked in the small cupboard with the sliding doors. Joan had even found time to run round the carpet with the sweeper. Altogether the little flatlet looked as pleasing as Elizabeth had ever seen it look, even when—which was more often than not—she had done all the chores herself.

'Everything as it should be, ma'am?' Joan demanded teasingly. 'I've put the groceries away, though I don't suppose they'll be exactly where you'd have put them, but it's not a large enough area for anything to be lost, is it? I've got a surprise as well,' she concluded triumphantly, turning to the screened-off shower and producing, to Elizabeth's delighted surprise, a small vase of plain white pottery with three alert-looking scarlet tulips, splashed boldly with gold, and a trailing spray of fern surrounding the whole.

'I won the Common Room Sweep this week,' Joan announced. 'I was saving it until we had a night off together, but somehow this seemed a more special occasion, if you get my meaning? I mean to say, all the others are used to coming in and finding my bits and pieces all over the place, and you fussing like a hen with one chick trying to keep the coop tidy, so I thought, as our Dr Lloyd hadn't been here before, it might make a bit of an impression on him—and on you too—if I rushed around a little first.' Her eyes twinkled, but Elizabeth knew she was waiting for approval. She had changed her dress into one of the dark colours which helped her look so much slimmer, and put some make-up on, and altogether she had really set out to make what she would have called 'a good impression'.

'It all looks lovely—and so do you—and how you've managed all this in the time I've been with Simmy I'll never know, but,' she added as she sensed the other's delight at this praise, 'I feel a bit of a pig leaving you to do it all!'

'You did the meal, and it was really my turn,' Joan commented, 'so I guess we're even. I've some coffee going, if you'd like a cup after all that strong tea I know you'll have been drinking at Simmy's. How you can stand it I just can't imagine. It's so strong it'd knock a horse out, the tannin that's in it, *and* he never seems to remember who's taking sugar and who isn't. It's usually too sweet—and too strong—for me, anyway, but I know you drink it and say nothing, rather than upset the poor chap. How's he doing, by the way? We don't seem to have heard much of him lately.'

'I think he'll be all right now,' Elizabeth said cautiously, 'providing he doesn't encounter anything that's likely to reawaken those dreadful memories. Staff Walters says Mr Ambrose regards him as one of his outstanding successes, and Sister OP says he's a different man from when he first came in to us. He only has to go once every six weeks now, so I think he should be OK.'

'Good.' Joan whirled round and produced a hot cup of coffee made exactly as Elizabeth liked it, not too milky, but with a little cream on top. 'You sit and relax,' she was beginning, when their doorbell pealed just once.

'I'll go,' Joan volunteered, and Elizabeth smiled, remembering how, when the television was switched on, Joan would have rather whoever it was had stood there ringing, ringing, ringing rather than miss one word or incident which was holding her attention.

She heard the voice of Dr Lloyd, fairly deep and sounding anxious, and Joan's reply, assuring him that everything was in order and that 'Nurse Fletcher has arranged for you to see Mr Simmonds . . . it's this way . . .', then she heard Joan inviting him to 'call in and let us know how it's gone!' before she returned inside the flat and closed the door.

'He'll be about half an hour, I guess,' Joan said briefly. 'I'd like to see the Manlay programme, if you don't mind.'

'Not a bit,' Elizabeth assured her, knowing Joan always watched it, and that she usually read. 'I'll get my book.'

They were each engrossed in their respective recreations when, about thirty minutes later, the door-bell pealed again, not waveringly this time, but with an imperative insistence which seemed to demand entry for whoever was outside.

Elizabeth glanced at Joan, but the hero was evidently in an intriguing situation, and her gaze remained on the flickering screen. Elizabeth murmured 'I'll go,' but she doubted if Joan heard.

It was a very different-looking Dr Lloyd who was standing on the doorstep.

'Thanks a million, Nurse!' he began, and to Elizabeth's utter astonishment he seized her hands and shook them vigorously. 'You just don't know what this means to us,' he began. 'When I telephone Ann she'll be thrilled. We expected to have to wait ages before we found anything else but a hotel bed-sitter, and they're too dashed expensive in the circumstances!'

What the circumstances were he didn't say, nor did Elizabeth feel she could enquire at this point. If he wished her to know, she thought, then he would tell her. Meanwhile, he'd have Mr. Simmonds coming up to find out what all the noise was about, and the Frazers, whose flat was across the corridor from that of the girls, would perhaps have some doubts about the wisdom, after all, of throwing up a settled life and home where they were for an unknown country, employment and unknown future friends.

'Won't you come inside and have a coffee to cele-brate?' she asked politely. 'Joan's just made some, and she's rather an expert.'

She had somehow expected him to refuse, but he accepted with an alacrity which surprised her. He must, she thought, have felt greatly in need of some sympathe-tic soul into whose willing ears he could spill the delight-ful story of a successful interview.

He looked round appreciatively as Joan, swaying slightly in an attempt to impress him with a gliding walk which was so different from her customary 'nurse's trot', that Elizabeth had to suppress a desire to laugh out loud. When he was finally settled in the largest of the three easy chairs, his coffee and a plate of biscuits on a small table beside him, Joan switched off the television—and Elizabeth guessed that particular programme had ended for the day—and settled herself opposite to him, smil-ing.

'Now we can chat,' she said firmly, exactly, Elizabeth thought with amusement, as though she had been the one to have insisted on the television being on and Joan had only been waiting for peace and quiet.

'You don't come from around here, do you, Dr Lloyd?' Joan, Elizabeth felt, had no inhibitions when she wanted to find out about anything or anyone.

'No,' he said after a moment or so of hesitation. 'I come from North Yorkshire. My father, and his father before him, had a general practice there. They expected . . . someone to carry on, but life doesn't always turn out the way we expect—or even hope—it will, don't you agree?'

'It sometimes, surprisingly enough, turns out better than if we each held the planning of it ourselves, I've found,' Elizabeth commented as no one else appeared to have anything to say. 'Do what one thinks is right, or what seems to be right at that particular time, and I find things often have a way of sorting themselves out from the most awful-seeming muddles.'

'I hope you're right—so far as I'm concerned, anyway,' he said with seeming deliberation, almost as though he were talking to himself, speaking his thoughts out aloud. 'I *had* to find a home for Mrs Lloyd—Ann,' he corrected himself quickly. 'And I hope they can do with a day nurse at St Jude's. She really needs to be occupied, and she's trained in all branches of nursing one can think of . . .'

'Sister Outpatients was saying she'll be needing a new staff nurse when Staff Collinson marries next month,' Joan put in, adding cautiously, 'is your . . . is Mrs Lloyd prepared to work as Staff OP, do you think?'

'I think, just at this moment,' Dr Lloyd seemed to be

choosing his words very carefully indeed, 'she would be prepared to do any nursing work which would enable her to . . . recover from a rather painful and drastic shock. I'd rather not talk any more about it just now, if you don't mind,' he said more quickly, once again the slightly agitated uncertain young man Joan had described him to be on first sight. 'Later, perhaps . . .'

'Of course.' Expertly Elizabeth took charge of the situation. She knew Joan's curiosity might very well get the better of her with no warning whatsoever, and suddenly she felt an overwhelming sympathy for the young man sitting back in his chair, his hands nervously holding his coffee cup and plate as though he anticipated dropping them without warning. She smiled at him as she spoke, and only Elizabeth, it seemed, didn't realise just how warming, how comforting her smile could be.

'Once she's settled in,' she began briskly, 'she'll soon find too much to do to have time to worry about whatever it is. Jude's is a busy hospital, and the OP's department is one of the busiest I've ever encountered. These flats don't look as though they're difficult to tend, but the two factories just outside town, although they don't make a smoke, thank goodness, seem somehow to *attract* the specks and bits and pieces which make housekeeping a little chore.'

'Ann's never been one for a great deal of housework,' he smiled slightly, as though at a memory. 'Is there a good library close by?' was his next question, 'and anywhere for music?'

'Library just around the corner,' Elizabeth told him. 'I go there a great deal, and Miss Hurst, the chief librarian, is most helpful. I don't know much about music, I'm afraid. I do know there is an amateur operatic society which attempts some wonderful productions and usually is highly successful with them! There is also some sort of Musical Appreciation Society, whatever that may be. Miss Hurst at the library can tell you all you'd need to know about whatever interests you, from books to the museum and the Fine Art Collection, of which the town is very proud.'

'She *ought* to be able to settle happily here,' Dr Lloyd startled them both by the unexpectedness of his remark, particularly as it was made in such a considering tone. 'And if she can work as well . . .'

Suddenly he seemed to realise he was speaking to two strangers, people he had only just met and who, presumably, would know nothing or, he comforted himself, very little of the lives of himself and Mrs Lloyd. He straightened his shoulders visibly and rose, placing the cup, saucer and plate with careful accuracy in the centre of the table.

'I must be off,' he said apologetically. 'I'm supposed to be on call in about an hour! I take it the flat we're to have is almost identical with yours?'

'Almost,' Elizabeth explained. 'It's like this but sort of in reverse, if you understand what I mean. That is, the fireplace is—or was, since they're all boarded up since the central heating was installed—on the opposite wall. The two flues shared a chimney or something like that. That, of course, puts their window where our fireplace boarding is. Apart from that, and the fact that they have an extra bedroom, they're more or less the same.'

'I did ask about the two bedrooms,' Dr Lloyd said, flushing. 'Have you the one only, then?'

'There were two small ones,' Joan didn't like being left out of the conversation and joined in with enthusiasm. 'We decided to have the partition moved, so that we've one large room which is big enough to take twin beds, two small wardrobes and equally small dressing-tables and gives each of us a feeling of independence! It also,' she grinned, 'has the advantage of giving us a slip of a room into which we cram anyone unfortunate enough to come to us on a prolonged visit, that is, to stay overnight or something like that.'

'You seem to have worked out all the angles,' he laughed. 'I've no doubt, being a woman, there'll be changes Ann will want to make. Does she hame to see Mr Simmonds about that?'

'Only if changes interfere with the structure of the flat,' Elizabeth told him. 'I shouldn't think she'll want to go in for anything very drastic, especially if you're both working, at least not until she's sort of found her bearings in the town, I mean.'

'If she stays as long as that'll take,' Dr Lloyd said gloomily, Joan decided, but with an abrupt change of manner, he turned to go, holding out a hand to each of them in turn.

'My name's Michael,' he said briskly. 'I think off duty, and as we are to be close neighbours, we might use christian names, don't you?'

They shook hands formally, Elizabeth feeling slightly foolish although she couldn't think why, then he turned to go, both girls accompanying him to the lift which was now operating again.

When they had called their final 'goodnight' and assured him he would have no difficulty in getting his Mini into the garage space previously occupied by the Frazers' car, he was gone.

'Well,' Joan sighed as she lowered herself into the

chair he had just vacated and put her feet on a low stool, 'it's a mystery, but there for all that! Indisputable!'

'What is?' Elizabeth didn't pause in her stacking and washing of the dishes and crockery they had used. Joan, she knew, would do nothing more this evening.

'That all the nice, comfortable and attractive men are married before one meets them!' Joan sighed prodigiously. 'It just isn't fair! There's Dr Lloyd, a most attractive man if he lost that air of being forlorn and had enough to eat, and he with a wife he doesn't even seem certain will stay around with him, after all the trouble he's taken to find this flat and everything! And then there's Dr O'Toole with never a serious word to be got out of him, and as ugly as the proverbial toad, thinking he's only to use that silver tongue of his to flatter and any girl, nurse or not, will fall over herself to go around with him in his rattly old banger! And never a bean will *he* have to his name, unless he wins the Irish Sweepstake, and who'd be seen—or heard—going around with *him*, I'd like to know? His laughter's like a bull bellowing, and he never seems to stop!'

'He's happy, anyway,' Elizabeth had finished the dishes and was smoothing hand-cream into her fingers. 'I'd say that's more than can be said of Dr Lloyd, poor soul! I wonder what's the matter?' she mused, more to herself than to Joan, but Joan, never silent for long together, took up the challenge immediately.

'Married on the rebound when he was a student, I shouldn't wonder,' she said cryptically. 'Seems to me he regrets it, as well.'

'That's something we don't know,' Elizabeth's tone was slightly rebuking. 'They could have had a child . . . and lost it. She could be ill . . .'

'Or it could be just our old friend "incompatibility" rearing his ugly head! Interesting! I'm dying to see what she's like.'

'None of our business, anyway,' Elizabeth closed the subject firmly, settling in her chair as Joan switched on the television set again. 'Pass my book, please, there's a love,' and apart from the sound of the dialogue and background noises of the play being presented, silence reigned in the little flat until time for bed.

CHAPTER TWO

THE first few days of the following week flashed by in the
sort of whirl Elizabeth remembered so well when she
had been accustomed to regular changeover.

It was good to be back on the wards again, and after
the first few hours she soon was back in the familiar
routine and it was almost as though she had never been
on Cas for such a long time now that it was almost
soothing to be once more on Women's Medical.

Almost, but not quite. There wasn't anything very
soothing about the way in which Michael Lloyd made his
round, for instance. Mary Worthington, looking quite
unlike her usual serene self in the new frilly cap of her
Senior Sistership, hovered about 'just like a bee round a
honey-pot', Elizabeth thought a little scornfully. She
was at once angry with herself. Such spitefulness, even
when not voiced aloud, was foreign to her nature, and
she strangely resented the fact that she could, apparently, give vent to it—mentally, at any rate—just as easily as
the next person.

'Stop it!' she admonished herself. 'Just because you
and Joan think there's some sort of mystery about the
man that's no reason to resent him from the very beginning! He seems pleasant enough.'

The patients appeared to like and to trust him on
sight. One old lady, a Mrs Elliot who had given no end of
trouble since she had been admitted as a suspected
diabetic, smiled toothlessly up into his face and declared

she was 'a sight better just from seeing someone different from that Dr Walsh.' To the astonishment of Elizabeth as well as to the evident surprise on the face of Sister Worthington, Dr Lloyd merely smiled and gave some light retort about a change, even of face, being as good as a rest, before he went on to the next bed.

Miss Johnson, the tracheitis, came in for observation, as did Mrs Robson, whose position had to be slightly changed before he was satisfied that the head was sufficiently in a downwards position to allow the postural drainage necessary.

Most of the other patients in the ward were given a friendly greeting during the brief inspection, rather than examination. He wrote up several prescriptions, had a word with Staff on one or more occasions, and finally halted at the bedside of Mrs Rentworth, whose lobar pneumonia showed a remarkable rise in toxaemia. He wrote a prescription, issued instructions, and seemed to give out such a feeling of confidence all at one and the same time that despite herself and her first faint misgivings Elizabeth felt her heart warm to him as she realised here was someone dedicated to give of his best to all who came under his care.

So much for his first day on the ward to which Change-Over had designated her! It set the tone of their workaday relationship as nearly perfectly as was possible, but the same could not as yet be said of life at Landawne House, the Victorian mansion which now housed a wider mixture of inhabitants than ever in its life before this.

On the Monday morning Elizabeth and Joan had almost been made late for Jude's, by the upsurge of departing Frazers and their family. Molly Frazer, white-faced and determined, as she was about to embark on what she fervently and audibly hoped would be the last crazy venture her husband would desire to make. Hovering around her, Ian, equally white-faced, was plainly determined this time as he always was when undertaking anything new, to succeed.

'I've told her over and over again, Nurse, you've heard me?' he appealed to Elizabeth. 'It was no fault of mine the last two people I've worked for have gone bankrupt! They'd put all they had into those ventures, poor souls. In most ways it's we who should be sorry for them! At least it hasn't landed us in a cartload of debt!'

'Small thanks to you—or them—if it had,' Molly said with a quite unexpected bitterness. 'We could see the way the wind was blowing months back! We ought to have guessed, after the first showdown, but no, "give him a chance", you kept saying. Only by pinching a penny here and a penny there did I manage enough for us to at least get off, fairly inexpensively, to a new start. And this time,' she added threateningly, 'it'd better work, if you want to keep us all together!'

'She's upset, Nurse. She doesn't mean what she says, not all of it, anyway,' he patted his wife's shoulder with a clumsy gesture which seemed only to irritate his wife further. 'She's never been far from her folks before this,' he added, 'but her parents are coming as soon as they can. They promised last night. Molly's dad's a good way off from being active, and as you know, her mum's one of the best dressmakers in the county. They'll do all right, and so shall we,' he concluded confidently, but as though the mention of her parents had broken the last thread of her self-control, Molly burst into loud and tearful sobs, completely nonplussing her husband.

'Slightly hysterical, and no wonder,' Elizabeth commented crisply to Joan. 'You put the kettle on, will you, pet? I'll take them in and make a fresh pot of tea if you'll run down and ask Simmy to phone for a taxi from the corner. It's the only way we'll make it by now, and we can borrow from the holiday fund and pay it back later.'

'It'll be two pounds, at least,' Joan commented, but not unkindly. 'You go and ask about phoning, you're better pals with Simmy than I am. I'll make the cuppa. You know I can do *that* without it taking tact or upsetting anything, though,' she warned, 'I won't have time to move the cups, remember!'

Elizabeth had departed to the basement, and when the necessary message had been phoned through she asked Mr Simmonds to collect her key when the other taxi arrived to take the Frazer family and their hand-luggage to the train which was to be the first part of their journey into a new life.

When she reached their flat again calm had been restored and a still semi-tearful Molly was full of apologies for her unexpected behaviour.

'It's true, Nurse,' she confided to Elizabeth, 'I've never left them for more than a train journey away, never in my life before, and it seems like looking forward for *ever* till I see them again! If we'd all gone together I wouldn't have minded. Now, what happens if either we or they are in a sea disaster?' she concluded woefully.

'I don't think I'd worry too much about *that* if I were you,' Elizabeth countered cheerfully. 'Think of all the folks who, just in these last few years, have crossed the Atlantic in all sorts of tiny craft, and without much hope of survival if anything *did* go wrong. You, and they, when they follow, will be on a stable, modern ship, as well maintained and handled as possible, and I believe that's something out of this world nowadays. How long before they're likely to follow you, any idea?'

'In about six months, they told them,' Ian answered for his wife. 'The man said it might be less than that, but certainly, if all goes well, it shouldn't take any longer than that!'

'And it's nine months to Christmas!' Elizabeth countered, smiling as Molly's woebegone countenance lightened. 'It doesn't seem five minutes since we were all rushing like mad to cope with the last festive season, so if you look at it like that, Molly love . . .'

She broke off and suddenly bent down to kiss the other woman.

'We shall miss you as neighbours,' she said sincerely, 'and I'm sure wherever you go you'll soon make friends and be just as happy as I think you've been here. I hope you will be, anyhow. Keep in touch, won't you?' she pressed. 'We shall want to know how you're all getting along, the children in particular! They'll be thrilled.'

She broke off as the taxi which was to convey herself and Joan to the hospital sounded a warning note from outside.

'Plenty of tea left in the pot,' she added. 'You know where the sugar and milk are kept, and there's a box of freshly-made buns and things in the kitchen. Leave the key with Mr Simmonds . . . cheerio, and the best of luck!'

They were off at last, just as a small furniture van pulled up outside Landawne House.

'Just our luck,' Joan grumbled good-naturedly as they settled back in the taxi. 'The Lloyds' furniture arriving just as we drive off! I'd love to know—in advance, so to speak—just what kind of taste they have, wouldn't you?'

'I'm not really interested,' Elizabeth was truthfully honest. 'To judge by Dr Lloyd I'd say it would be purely utilitarian in character, but she may be very different. As she'll obviously be handling their domestic affairs I should think a great deal will depend on what her tastes are, rather than his.'

'Should be mutual!' Joan asserted, 'but I imagine things so seldom are!'

'I really wouldn't know,' Elizabeth said absently. She had no experience of the married state, and so far as she was concerned she was perfectly convinced that when or if she married the partner of her choice would be as reasonable as she was herself, and all such mundane matters would have been ironed out well before they set up a home together. At the moment she was more concerned with arriving at St Jude's on time than with anything or anyone else.

They were on time, thanks to the driver's knowledge of the back streets of the busy market town, and his quick thinking which twice helped them avoid being held up for long spells in traffic jams. Senior Sister Worthington, Elizabeth knew, was famed for being what the staff called 'a bit testy' in the morning, and it was a relief to find herself in the ward and able to take her part in the changeover from the night staff.

The day was as busy as it could be. There were three new admissions, two people had to be placed on the DI list and be specialled, Nurse Wyburn had to be taken off duty as she became suddenly ill with, according to Dr Blake, the house physician, a suspected appendicitis. Sister Fletcher, as Elizabeth was gradually becoming accustomed to thinking of herself, was kept hard at it throughout the day, and when she met Joan, this being one of the all-too-infrequent days on which they could journey home together, she was feeling so tired she had begun to wonder if, after all, the promotion was worth the effort involved.

'Cheer up,' Joan advised comfortingly. 'At least no one's suggested you live in at the Nurses' Home, have they? If they do then I'll have to move back too, and we'd not even be on the same floor any more. Do you think you can keep this up, Liz? I'll do more than my share in the flat if that'll help.'

'I know you will, pet, and we'll manage somehow,' Elizabeth smiled, but just then she was far too tired to even think more seriously about the idea. 'I don't want to go back to living in the Home, pleasant though it is. I like being on our own, so it ought to be worth while making any little extra bit of effort involved, but we'll see.'

'Especially with that nice Dr Lloyd as our new neighbour,' Joan murmured irrepressibly. 'We know there's a Mrs Lloyd, but she's not even been seen as yet, so she can't be as important as all that! And anyhow, they're bound to have friends something like themselves and connected with our sort of world.'

'Still determined to marry and raise a crowd of nurses and potential doctors, are you, love?' Elizabeth raised a smile as they reached their stop. 'Don't know why you bother. There's a lot more to living than all that sort of thing. Look at the divorce rate, for instance. That's hardly an encouragement for anyone thinking in terms of a family-type future.'

'There's always been something in the way of true love, ultimate happiness and what-have-you, hasn't there?' Joan retorted with an undisturbed composure. 'I should think in the old days—and I mean the really long-ago-type old days—when girls were more or less handed over to the highest bidder or a man married a well-dowered girl had their impediments too. Then there were the Victorian days, with all that subtle class-consciousness and snobbery. I think love of any sort has a better—and more honest—chance of survival these days than it's ever had before!'

'You may be right,' Elizabeth commented, reversing her usual custom of walking upstairs and ringing for the small automatic lift instead, a fact which surprised Joan more than she would have admitted had anyone asked her to comment. 'I suppose, like a great many other difficult things in life, it could well be "all in the mind" so to speak. Listen!'

She paused dramatically in the wide corridor outside their own small flat. From somewhere close at hand they heard the sound of a piano being played, and played with the touch of a master, but the music sounded to contain all the sadness in the world, so that, listening, Elizabeth shivered involuntarily.

'What—or who—is that?' she whispered.

'A piano.' Joan was as prosaic and as matter-of-fact as ever, adding with a brisk reproof in her tone, 'but whoever it is I wish they'd play something a little more cheerful! That's enough to give anyone the willies, especially after a hard day.'

'Chopin prelude in E minor,' Elizabeth murmured. 'And Chopin hadn't really a great deal about which to make particularly joyful music, you know.'

'I didn't, as a matter of fact,' Joan paused, listening. There was silence for a moment, then the music began again, but this time it was a song with orchestral accompaniment, a song which Elizabeth failed to recognise this time but which Joan immediately began to sing softly, under her breath.

'Sounds like a record player, and whoever's playing it is a pretty wretched person, by the sound of things.'

'Must be . . .' Elizabeth began, and paused, but Joan had no inhibitions about such matters and finished the sentence for her.

'Mrs Lloyd,' she said quietly. 'She must have arrived while we've been at work. She sounds very unhappy . . . listen, she's back on that Prelude or whatever you called it! I'd like to pop over and lend her something more cheerful.'

Elizabeth, who did not altogether share her friend's tastes in music, smiled gently.

'She might be grateful,' she said, opening the door to their own flat, more than a little worried that someone might come along and find the pair of them obviously listening to the music which someone was quite evidently playing as a help towards his or her own peace of mind.

'On the other hand,' she continued reflectively, 'it may well be she just has a thing about that particular tune. Some people do have feelings along those lines, you know!'

'Time she shook herself out of it, then,' was Joan's crisp comment as she followed her companion inside and shut the door. Even with their own door closed they could still plainly her the plaintive, haunting music which seemed to be the very voice of a soul in torment, crying, pleading to be understood, to find sympathy and without reward.

'I can't stand it!' Joan exploded violently as the recording started again. 'I'll just have to have something cheerful to listen to, sorry and all that, love, but whoever's playing on here'll be a sight more with it than *that*!'

The cheery, blatant sound of some television jingle advertising some form of deodorant rent the air. Elizabeth visibly shuddered. For her own choice she would have greatly preferred the mournful Chopin or the dirge-like orchestrated piece which, it seemed, had been transformed into a popular song.

'Sorry about that, love,' Joan apologised, and turned down the volume to a point which was relatively bearable. 'It's just that the thing she's playing is getting on my nerves . . .'

'Nurses have no business to have "nerves" of that sort!' Elizabeth mocked Sister Worthington so successfully that Joan laughed aloud, her temporary ill-humour forgotten. Elizabeth, expertly dishing up the 'lamb chops suprême', a favourite quick recipe of hers, smiled again, leaving Joan to the contemplation of the television programme as she continued to lay the table for two, but her own ears were strained to listen to the plaintive music from across the corridor, and she was more than a little disturbed to hear the Prelude record started up yet once again, although sounding far away now with the voices from the picture screen obtruding into the room as well.

Neither of them mentioned Mrs Lloyd throughout their simple meal. Joan was still intently watching the screen, and Elizabeth was still, and with equal intensity, listening to the sounds from Flat Five.

'She must be dreadfully unhappy,' she thought, and tried hard to remember whether or not Dr Lloyd was on call that evening or not. Jude's, she felt, had the best system of any hospital in which she had worked as yet, or of which she had heard. Although most of the medical staff lived in, none of them was on call every night, and there was a very fair rota which seemed to give as much free time as could possibly be arranged so that those who wished to continue their studies could do so. Others, less ambitious, were glad enough of the extra free time in which to relax and enjoy life a little.

Into which category did Dr Lloyd fall? Elizabeth wondered. If it were the former, then how could he possibly devote any time to study, to research or whatever it was in particular in which he was interested, with that mournful sound ringing in his ears?

If it were the latter, then surely he would have arranged to take Mrs Lloyd out somewhere on her first evening in her new home? Malenchester wasn't a swinging town by any means, but there were three cinemas, a theatre where amateur companies—and the occasional professional one—showed something of interest each week.

'There's the Green Goddess,' she remembered, 'and the Golden Slipper, each with cabaret and music. Dancing at the Casino, and there's always the Giant's Walk if she's the outdoor type!' she remembered, thinking of the strange line of almost flat rocks which crowned the highest hillside in the locality. 'Surely she wouldn't really want to spend her first evening in a new place just mooning away over a couple of records—which appear to be all they possess!'

She looked at the joint collection of records owned by Joan and herself. Whatever Mrs Lloyd's tastes in music might prove to be Elizabeth was certain she would find something of interest somewhere amongst the pile.

'I wonder if I ought to pop across and ask if she'd like to borrow a few of them?' Elizabeth mused to herself. 'I know back home Mother always talks about making newcomers welcome, but there's a great deal of difference in living in Pursley Mackton in a cottage-cum-house where one's family has lived for generations, and in living in a huge house divided into flatlets, where so little is known about anyone else in the place except the caretaker and his wife! I'd like her to feel welcome . . . after all, it was because of young Tim falling downstairs on their first day here that we came to know the Frazers so well and so quickly. We can't expect anything like that where there's just Dr and Mrs Lloyd . . .'

She toyed with the idea for some minutes, Joan being lost in the adventures of some private detective or other who appeared, at the moment to be in grave danger of losing his life as well as his 'case'. Elizabeth wasn't interested. It would all work out right in the end, she knew, and therefore she wasn't interested. Real life, she felt, held drama enough and to spare, without the make-believe drama on which Joan and so many other people appeared to survive. Elizabeth was interested in *people*, but the people had to be real and alive, not shadows on a screen or printed words in a book before they aroused and held her interest.

There was a commercial on now to which Joan had taken a dislike some weeks previously, and she turned down the volume until the chatter was ended. In the sudden quiet the notes of the Prelude sounded quite clearly, and that helped Elizabeth to make up her mind.

'I won't be a minute,' she said, getting up and crossing

to the door. 'I'm just going to see if there's anything we can do.'

She had closed the door quietly behind her before Joan was out of her chair. It was, perhaps, a little unfair to walk out like this, for Joan, she knew, was dying of curiosity about Mrs Lloyd. Curiosity was one thing, but Elizabeth knew this wasn't her own real motive for a call. Something, she didn't know what, but some sort of hunch nagged her to cross the corridor and to tap on the door. Maybe, she reflected as she waited for someone to answer her quiet knock, there was something she could do, maybe not, but at least she would have the satisfaction of doing her best to be helpful.

It appeared at first her knock would be ignored, but just as she raised her hand to repeat the summons the door opened a cautious few inches and a young woman's face looked out.

Elizabeth's first reaction was one of astonished pity. The face was youthful, but the eyes seemed to hold all the age-old tragedies of the world. The oval shape of the face was clear and almost devoid of make-up or of any attempt to make the best of what were really extremely attractive features, but the eyes were what captured and held Elizabeth's attention above all else. They were dark brown, in contrast with the pale honey-gold hair which swung loosely about the too-thin face, and in those eyes was such utter desperation and longing that, without any reason whatsoever, Elizabeth felt herself to be an intruder.

'I'm Nurse Fletcher,' she began, holding out her hand. 'I live in the flat opposite. I work with Dr Lloyd at Jude's. We—that is the nurse who shares the flat with me, and myself—wondered if there was anything we could do to make you feel welcome. Have you bread, milk . . . everything you need? There's no necessity to stand on ceremony. Just say . . . and we'll help if we can.'

There was a pause and a silence which Elizabeth felt she could have cut with a knife, then the other spoke, not smiling, but with a cool detachment as though the flat, the neighbours, the state of her larder and prospect of a meal had nothing whatsoever to do with Mrs Lloyd herself.

'Thank you,' she said in a melodious but quiet voice. 'There's nothing anyone can do . . . not now. Good-night.' Before Elizabeth had recovered from the shock the door was quietly but firmly closed and she heard the key being turned inside. Before she was back at her own door the plaintive sound of the Prelude was heard again, and she turned away, her heart suddenly overwhelmed with sadness for whatever the tragedy of the other woman might be, even though she did not know her.

Elizabeth was thoughtful as she returned—more slowly—to her own door. She was thankful she, and not Joan, had been the one to make the first tentative venture towards friendliness with Mrs Lloyd.

Easy-going though Joan was by nature, a rebuff such as Elizabeth had just received would have sent her somewhat uncertain temper flaring into some sort of practically unforgivable retort, one which might well have made an enemy of their new neighbour instead of the friend they had hoped for.

'She's dreadfully unhappy,' Elizabeth mused, quietly opening her own door. 'There's no sound of anyone there but herself—I'm sure Dr Lloyd's not been home all evening, and the only sound we've heard from there has been that record player, and just the two tunes. I wish I'd asked her if she would have liked to borrow some of ours . . .'

'What's she like?' Joan turned from the fascination of the television as the programme changed to a documentary in which she was not interested. 'Is she pretty? Old, young, fat, thin . . .? What *is* she like?' she said half teasingly.

Elizabeth paused for a moment. One half of her mind was fully occupied with the mental picture of that lovely, sad face as it peered through the door, and the other half searching for words which would convey, without seeming stupid, the hopeless feeling of inadequacy which had assailed her when she had met with such an unexpected but deliberate rebuff.

'About our ages, I'd say,' she managed, aware that Joan was staring curiously at her. 'She's not pretty exactly, she's really rather lovely, but in an odd sort of way. She looks like one of those Madonnas one sees in the old-time frescoes and so on. She's too thin, and she'd be lovely—if she took any sort of trouble with herself. It's obvious that she isn't in the least interested as to how she looks, and her eyes are among the most beautiful I've ever seen . . . but as sad and lonely as any eyes I've ever seen.'

'Charming!' Joan said cryptically. 'That tells me a lot! What did she say?'

'She didn't say anything, not really,' Elizabeth confessed. 'I asked if there was anything at all we could do, and she said . . . "there isn't anything anyone can do . . . not now", as though something *could* have been done at some point in the past, and no one had bothered.'

'I shouldn't worry,' Joan shrugged the matter off with an ease which Elizabeth envied, but Joan, she reflected, hadn't seen the infinite sadness in those huge brown eyes! 'Pop the kettle on, will you, love, before you sit down?'

And that, Elizabeth reflected as she did as she had been asked, was evidently that! Joan returned, undisturbed, to her contemplation of the flickering screen, and Elizabeth to her book, only looking up with a murmured word of thanks when Joan presented her with another cup of coffee she really didn't want.

It was as she returned off duty two evenings later that Elizabeth was overtaken on the stairs by Dr Lloyd. The lift was out of order—again—but he, like the rest of the tenants of the converted house, appeared not to mind very much.

'I hoped I'd see you, Nurse,' he began a little breathlessly. 'Ann starts work at St Jude's on Monday. She'll be Staff OP, and I have a feeling, somehow, I've you to thank for this! Anyhow,' he cut short her protestations with a gesture, 'whoever is responsible they don't realise just how much they've helped her. It isn't doing her any good at all to just sit around the flat, moping. It's as well we all aren't the same way inclined when life gives us a rough deal, don't you think, Nurse?'

Elizabeth looked startled. This almost bordered on being confidential, and the last thing she wanted, or felt she wanted, at this stage, was to be burdened with any more confidences from anyone else. Joan had said on more than one occasion, 'You have a faculty of finding lame dogs and making them go over the stile, even if they don't want to, love. It's time you stopped it, before you become a managing woman!'

'I don't know much about it, I'm afraid,' she said now, almost apologetically, and although it might well have been her imagination it seemed he looked at her in a surprised manner.

'There's the monthly dance at the Nurses' Home on Wednesday of next week,' she blurted out, quite without knowing she was going to mention that event. 'I don't often go to them nowadays—though I expect now I've been on Change-Over I might well start again, I don't know, but they're good fun, and one gets to know people . . .'

'Sounds an excellent idea,' he seemed amused. 'Might I ask if you've made up your mind whether or not you'll be at the one next Wednesday?'

'I . . . I haven't made up my mind yet,' Elizabeth said, annoyed because, for some unknown reason, she felt herself blushing. 'Joan always goes, so if Mrs Lloyd wanted someone to go with, someone who'd introduce her around so to speak, then Joan would be glad to help her find friends.'

'I'll tell Ann,' he said gravely, 'but I don't hold out much hope of her agreeing to go! It would do her good, though, so I'll do my best to persuade her. She might,' he added somewhat inconsequentially Elizabeth thought, 'go if *you* were going as well . . . ?'

Remembering the pale, sad face which had looked so forlornly at her through the half-open door of the flat opposite, Elizabeth very much doubted the authenticity of this statement. Perhaps he was trying to be friendly, flattering her a little in the belief that this might persuade her to go round and ask Mrs Lloyd herself.

'I'll see' she half-promised vaguely. 'We'll talk about it afterwards. Maybe after a day on OP she won't want to go out in the evening, but sometimes it helps to get to know the people one's working with more or less. Out-Patients seems somehow cut off from the rest of us. Cas seemed like that at first. They're not, not really. It's just a sort of feeling one gets—I do, anyhow. Maybe, as you said, it's as well we aren't all alike in our feelings, Doctor!'

She was smiling faintly as she let herself into their flat and began preparations for the evening meal. This time she had let herself go, as Joan would have phrased it, not buying and preparing all fresh food herself, but, for the first time, sampling the excellent choice of delectables arrayed in the new 'Deep-Freeze' shop which had just opened in the new arcade on the outskirts of the town.

Elizabeth had bought deep-frozen plaice, frozen chipped potatoes, frozen green peas and a luscious-looking couple of extras, which she was not at all certain she didn't already regret, a carton of frozen strawberries and a carton of cream.

'What's all this, then?' Joan pushed open the door as the scent of the now frying plaice assailed her nostrils. 'Have you gone completely insane, or is this just your new way of showing me you *can* find time to open a few packets instead of poring over your cook-book for hours and ending with just as appetising a result? It all looks gorgeous,' she surveyed the almost ready meal. 'Doesn't this prove what I've been telling you for years? It's old-fashioned to carry on the way you do, trying to do all the shopping, veg cleaning, potato peeling and fruit preservation by yourself when there are all these wonderful things just on hand, ready to serve whenever you want them, and with a minimum of effort?'

'I'd rather be old-fashioned,' Elizabeth commented,

stirring briskly at something in a small pan. 'I think you may well agree with me when you taste this sauce.'

'And if I do, then of course, that's what'll have "made" the meal, I suppose?' Joan teased. 'I know I'm an ignoramus about these things, Liz, but I do feel you spend far too much time worrying about having everything just right! Who cares whether the food comes from a package or is freshly pulled, killed or what-have-you? I'm sure I don't, providing it's food, and edible, and tasty! That's all I require, and for the amount you eat it really can't make any difference one way or the other, except, maybe, to a calorie or two, and I don't suppose the few you manage to get over your required allowance really matter, not when you stop to think about it?'

'It matters, as you put it, to *me*,' Elizabeth said firmly, pouring the sauce into a small sauce-boat and planting it on the table with a flourish. 'That's one of the things I don't like about living in modern times. Everything's either ready-mixed, do-it-yourself or "follow simple directions on packet to achieve perfect results", and I don't feel that's really living.'

'For someone like me whose buns emerge like cannon balls and whose pastry never mixes properly, these things are a blessing,' Joan was philosophical about the whole business. 'I'm very much afraid, though, if ever I do manage to discover my dream man I'll have to take a cookery course before signing on the dotted line, or whatever it is one has to do to tie the knot!'

'I imagine there's a great deal more to it than that,' Elizabeth laughed, 'but I've no doubt whatsoever you'd manage as well as anyone else has ever done. It's always been my conviction that when two people love each other enough to be prepared to spend the rest of their lives together, each should be prepared for some minor adjustments, some rearrangement of their present mode of living, and in your case, the obvious thing is to learn some good, plain cooking. You can always experiment with the "fancy-work" once you're established, so to speak.'

'Doesn't sound very romantic,' Joan pulled a small face, 'but if I married anyone as prosaic as Dr Walsh, for instance, I suppose it would work . . . or perhaps it would be more correct to say it *might* work. Now Tim . . .'

'Tim?' Elizabeth began to laugh, not unkindly, but with sincere amusement. 'Don't tell me you've at last got around to calling our bouncing Irish lad by his christian name?'

'I did agree that it was foolish to carry on being so very formal if he's going to accompany me to the Wednesday hop,' Joan said primly. 'I said you might come along . . .' her voice trailed into silence, but Elizabeth shook her head.

'Not this month, I think,' she said decisively. 'Maybe next, but there's a good turn you could do for Dr Lloyd and Mrs Lloyd if you cared to, that is,' she added. 'I think he'd like her to get to know more of the staff members on a friendly basis. It takes time, as we know, but she seems so lost and out on a limb, and it seems to worry him more than unduly.'

'And you want me to suggest she goes along with us, with Tim and myself, on our very first date together?' Joan asked incredulously. 'I'll ask him, of course . . .'

'I didn't mean quite that,' Elizabeth hastened to explain, and then, not quite sure of what it was she really wanted Joan to do, tried again. 'Couldn't you suggest you meet her there, introduce her to a few people and so on? He knows most of the staff as he's in daily contact with most of them, but out on OP she'll see much less of anyone else except Sister Langdon and the doctors when it's their turn for any certain clinic. She's bound to feel lonely, especially if she's been working amongst friends for some time.'

'Who says she has?' Joan countered quickly, and Elizabeth was compelled to admit she knew nothing of the kind as a certainty.

'It's just . . . it seemed to me to be something like that,' she admitted, 'and whatever the reason she left— and presumably why Dr Lloyd left too—was something connected with whatever people keep referring to mysteriously as "the tragedy", and that this had some connection with either their work or their friends or both.'

'Sounds like a mystery thriller, if you ask me,' Joan grumbled, but her generous good-nature soon overcame her mild grumbles. 'I'll pop across now and ask if they'd like to join us' she said with a return to her normal generously-minded attitude towards others. 'Sure you won't change your mind and come too? Dr Blake's a great fan of yours, as if you didn't know! and Mr Ambrose would be sure to attend if he knew his favourite nurse was to be present!'

'It's more than a year since I worked with Mr Ambrose,' Elizabeth spoke quickly, but the colour rose in her cheeks as she recalled the teasing she had undergone from her fellow-nurses on the subject of Mr Ambrose.

'He's trying psychological techniques on you, Liz,' had been one of the favourite ones.

'He'll have you tranquilised and you won't know what you're agreeing to,' had been another. Elizabeth hadn't found them amusing. Paul Ambrose was a quiet, self-assured man of early middle-age, and she had both liked and admired him. He was easy to work with, kind and considerate, and she had really enjoyed his courteous attentions until the prolonged teasing had made her more than usually aloof. When she had been moved from his department, three Change-Overs ago now, she had at first felt regretful and resentful, but gradually that feeling had worn off. Their off-duties seldom coincided, and over the months she had seen very little of him.

Had she minded? Elizabeth wasn't sure. She had *liked* him well enough, perhaps more than any other man she had been out with, but never a gregarious type of person, she reflected that the number of her escorts could be counted on the fingers of her two hands.

'I don't, somehow, feel he was The One,' she reminded herself, bringing her mind back to the present with a conscious effort.

'I'm not going this time,' she said firmly. 'I've asked for an early vacation date, and I want to make some holiday dresses and things. I've more than enough to do as it is. I *might* come next month, if I break the back of all the sewing and whatnot I've got planned. I promised Mum I'd run up a couple of frocks for the twins as well, before they're home from school. That doesn't give me a great deal of free time!'

'OK. You're the boss of your own free time, anyway,' Joan said, hauling herself from the depths of the chair with an effort. 'Now, keep your fingers crossed for me! I saw Mrs Lloyd in the lift this morning, and she gave me the frostiest nod possible when I said "hello," and "how do you like Malenchester?'' She didn't seem to want to know me, but,' she added charitably, 'perhaps that's just her way.'

'She's unhappy,' Elizabeth stated the fact flatly. 'I wish I knew why. It's no business of mine, but Dr Lloyd seems to really put himself out to make her happy, and yet she doesn't look as though anything in life will ever interest her . . . again.'

'Why . . . again?' Joan asked curiously.

'Something she said,' Elizabeth thought back, recalling perfectly the lovely face and the sad brown eyes. 'I had the impression that, perhaps not so long ago, everything had been as nearly perfect as is possible in this world, and that somehow, and perhaps without rhyme or reason, everything that mattered had come to a halt, and she hadn't been able to get around to picking up the pieces, as it were.'

'Pieces of what?' Joan asked, mystified. Elizabeth smiled.

'An expression, love,' she had been quoting Paul Ambrose almost without knowing it. 'Pieces of her life as it had been before whatever bombshell struck it really hit her. That's all.'

'Sounds odd,' Joan shrugged. 'Anyway, I'll just pop across and see if they'd like to join Tim and me. Tim's lively enough company for anyone. Whatever's bothering her ladyship won't be allowed to interfere with the fun of the evening, if Tim has anything to do with it!'

She was gone before Elizabeth could reply, but something in her heart cried out to call after Joan to be careful in her handling of Mrs Lloyd. She didn't know what made her so certain the other woman was in need of help of some kind, of sympathy, of something more than, for all his obvious care of her, was missing from her companionship with Dr Lloyd.

'I don't *have* to meddle,' Elizabeth reminded herself. 'She's not a "case", she's a neighbour.'

Joan was back so quickly that instinctively Elizabeth feared the worst. Twin spots of colour burned in the other girl's cheeks, and her normally placid expression was one of bewildered anger.

'She doesn't have to be quite so rude, I suppose, does she?' Joan demanded as she closed the door. 'Maybe their life together isn't all it might be, maybe she's lost someone dear to her, maybe . . . all sorts of things, but politeness doesn't cost anything. All I did was ask if she and Dr Lloyd would care to come to the dance, but she didn't let me get any further . . .'

'Well?' Elizabeth asked as Joan paused for breath. 'What *did* she say?'

'She said she had no wish to socialise. She said that being too friendly with the people one worked with had upset her life too much already, and that she wasn't prepared to risk anything else happening. What do you suppose she means, Liz? Somehow I don't see Dr Lloyd getting too friendly with one of the nursing staff where they've been, do you? He doesn't seem that sort of man, and anyway, he's obviously devoted to her, though heaven alone knows why!'

The concluding part of the sentence was uttered in tones of such deep disgust that Elizabeth laughed despite the grave expression on her companion's face.

'It may not have been anything at all like that, you know,' she remarked reasonably. 'Everyone isn't too fond of tripping the light fantastic after a hard day on OP, or on the wards, for that matter! I definitely have to be in the mood for it myself, and I must admit that doesn't happen so very often these days.'

'You do act as though you're still alive, though,' Joan protested. 'They don't. He does when he's at work. At home the poor man looks as though he daren't call his soul his own! I bet he's henpecked!'

'You don't know, and neither do I,' Elizabeth said firmly, 'just what is wrong in that household, but I must admit,' she frowned, 'there does appear to be something most dreadfully wrong. She goes to work on the bus every morning—the one before that we catch when we don't walk—and she comes home alone each evening. He sleeps in most nights. I know he's on call, but it seems pretty pointless to go to the added expense of a flatlet, even one as minute as these places, if he doesn't intend to spend any time there at all. And when he's off duty they don't go out. She just plays those two records over and over again until the sound nearly drives me wild. I think it's having something of the same effect on Dr Lloyd. I've noticed once the record starts up it's not long before he's off, walking down the avenue as though he's in a hurry to get away.'

'I'm glad you've noticed that too,' Joan commented. 'I began to think I was imagining things. Well,' she tossed her head slightly, dismissing the Lloyds and their problems in the gesture, 'I shan't bother about them any more, and if you're wise you won't either! They'll come to us if they want anything, most folks do. Just you wait and see.'

Elizabeth made no comment, but she was saddened by the thought of the two new neighbours being so unhappy. The Frazers had been such a happy family. They had experienced their ups and downs, as do all families, but they had been happy, and their happiness had radiated throughout the building, infecting others who came into contact with them.

In just the same way, but in reverse, the unhappiness of the Lloyds appeared to be affecting the other tenants of Landawne House. Bill had commented on it when Elizabeth had gone down to the basement to ask him to repair a switch.

'I'll see to it in the morning, nurse,' he had promised as, after the inevitable cup of tea and chat he saw her to the door. 'Wish that record player or whatever it is in number five'd blow a fuse! I shouldn't be in any hurry to do a spot of repair work there, I can assure you. Fair gets on my nerves, just them two tunes and never a lighter song or nothin' to cheer a body up. Don't you think you could register a complaint, miss? Might help me to get her to shut it off a bit now and again.'

'It's not really loud,' Elizabeth objected, feeling a traitor to Joan as well as to herself, 'and it sounds so . . . *unhappy*,' she concluded. 'I'm sure, whatever the reason, it brings some sort of consolation to Mrs Lloyd for something about which we know nothing, and *you* know there are often things one can't explain to other people which are none the less real to the one concerned!'

'That's true enough,' Bill admitted, brightening. 'If anyone'll be able to help her, then it's you, Nurse, and I'd say that to anyone who asked me! We'll leave it alone, then, and wait and see. Mr Ambrose is a great believer in that sort of thing, isn't he?'

'In certain cases, yes!' Elizabeth smiled, 'and until we know for certain this isn't one of those cases I suggest we leave well alone, at least for a time?'

So it was agreed. The evening of the dance came and went. The Lloyds—and Elizabeth—stayed at home. The weeks drifted by, and Elizabeth and Joan went to the cinema twice, once to a play and once to a musical evening, and to the latter two entertainments they extended an invitation to the Lloyds, but Dr Lloyd was on duty on both occasions and Mrs Lloyd expressed a complete lack of interest.

Elizabeth attended the next monthly dance and thoroughly enjoyed herself. She missed the April one, expecting to be due for Change-Over, but when the time for the May dance approached Joan was insistent.

'There's that new Dr Bickersley,' she explained, 'the one who started on May the first. I'd like to get to know him better, he seems such a lively, light-hearted sort of person, and Tim gets so annoyed if I seem to be paying attention to anyone else but himself! Stupid things! If he'd any sense at all he'd realise I shouldn't be looking at anyone else if I knew for sure he *was* serious, but I never know where I am with him.'

'And you want to make friends with someone else who seems just like him?' Elizabeth twinkled, but Joan laughed, blushing a little.

'That's not the idea at all,' she said firmly, 'and well you know it! No, just you come along and when the dance gets going chat him up a little, draw him into the company, sort of thing. He's in Mr Scott's team, like Tim, so they know one another. Tim's going to ask him to come along, anyway, and even if you don't want to bother about getting to know him yourself, you might at least help me to make Tim see I *can* be attractive to someone else when I set my mind to it!'

'All right,' Elizabeth agreed reluctantly, 'so long as

I'm not dragged into your schemes! I'll work out my own fate when I'm good and ready, but if you think it's any use my trying to lend a hand with yours, I'll have a shot . . . just this once!'

CHAPTER THREE

By the time May the tenth was almost upon them, Joan seemed to have made up her mind that, once Elizabeth consented to appear at the monthly dance, all would be well with herself and Tim O'Toole.

It was useless for Elizabeth to protest and say she scarcely knew the man, much less the newcomer, Dr Bickersley. She had encountered him once or twice, but on a medical ward it was not very likely she would have a great deal to do with the orthopaedic surgeon and his team.

'I'll come to the dance, I promise,' she said at length in response to Joan's repeated urgings, 'but I promised to do a little shopping for Miss Lister first. Only in the new precinct, but it's so difficult for her to get about these days.'

'She'd be a great deal better off in a Home,' Joan opined quietly. 'There isn't a soul in the world belonging to her, and she depends on you for all the odds and ends she wants, or thinks she wants. I don't think she's short of cash, thank goodness. She ought to be able to get in somewhere where they'll look after her, and she wouldn't be a bother to anyone.'

'She isn't that as it is,' Elizabeth said quietly. 'She'd pine in a Home, no matter how good the Home was, the staff or the care they gave her. She lives for her window boxes and her two cats and that small bird of hers. It would be cruel to take her away from them now. All that's wrong with her is age.'

'And infirmity,' Joan said briefly. 'Face it, Liz. She's got arthritis, and well you know it. She's too far gone for any of the new developments to be of any use to her at all, except to relieve her of some of her pain, and she should be thankful enough for that! It's more than could have been done fifty years ago, with anyone as ill as she is.'

'It's more than could have been done twenty years ago,' Elizabeth agreed, 'but that doesn't make it any better for her, does it? She's happy where she is. I've asked about the District Nurse calling in, and that's going to be arranged, although just as yet there's little she can do. Miss Lister is very independent, as you know. She manages very well, once she's up and dressed, but it *is* difficult for her to get downstairs and along the street. Traffic confuses her, too. I only hope when I'm over eighty I'll manage one half as well as she's managing right now!'

'You will, love!' Joan grinned. 'You'll be all efficiency, and, in all probability, boss of your own hospital! You'll have all the help and assistance you'll ever need, and the best medical attention as well. You're fortunate, you know, just as I am. But I'll end up Granny to a squad of youngsters, and surely, even allowing for the present-day trend of putting the elderly out of the way as soon and as painlessly as possible, one or the other of them'll look after me . . . It must,' she added with unexpected wistfulness, 'have been much more satisfactory in the old days, when one expected one's grandparents or even one's great-grandparents to live with one after marriage. You know, sort of one great big happy family. I believe there are some countries where they still do that sort of thing, but I'm not sure where.'

'India, mainly, I believe,' Elizabeth smiled. 'On the other hand there are other "civilisations" where, when the old become a nuisance, they're popped out into the wilds and left until either the wild beasts do a disposal job or until the old folk die of exposure.'

'What a morbid subject!' Joan giggled. 'Let's get on to something more pleasant and to do with ourselves and the present! What are you going to wear on Saturday night?'

'My French blue, I think,' Elizabeth considered. 'I like pastel blues with dark hair, not that it matters,' she grinned impishly. 'I'm only the modern version of a chaperone, I know, so it doesn't really matter what I wear, but the rose seems to have seen more monthly dances than I can remember!'

'I'm down to my lime-green, I suppose,' Joan said ruefully. 'That's the thing with my shade of hair! Nothing goes with it.'

'Rubbish!' Elizabeth eyed the mane of shining bronze which Joan had released from the confines of her cap and which now lay on her shoulders in a shining but straight mass. 'Why don't you let Angela see what she can do? Have it shampooed, styled and set in a different way. I'd think if you had it piled high and wore your dark green you'd look lots slimmer and taller. Try it. And then pop into Isobel's next door and let them see what they can suggest in the way of a complete change of make-up. You never know, it might bring a turn of luck, if that's what you're really wanting.'

There was silence for a moment as Joan appeared to be giving the matter her fullest consideration. Then she spoke.

'I don't know what I want, not really, Liz,' she said at

last. 'I mean, I know I want to be married, to have a home and someone to care for—and who'll care for me too, of course—but that's not the whole of it. You're all right. You're slim and lovely. You've a lovely clear complexion. I don't think I remember ever seeing you with a spot or a pimple in all your life at Jude's. You walk well, and talk well, and one way and another you seem to . . . well, I don't mean this in any nasty fashion, but you seem to have, as though by some unknown right, all the things which go to make up a popular, well-sought-after girl. And you couldn't care less!'

She sounded so aggrieved that, despite her woebegone tones, Elizabeth laughed outright.

'You could have all those same advantages and more, if you took a little trouble,' she said confidently. 'You don't make the most of yourself to begin with. You won't discipline yourself either, as a second thing. You have to do something like that right from the start, you know, love. It just doesn't come by itself. Not all of it. And you were born with a number of advantages I don't possess and never will, believe it or not!'

'Such as?' Joan demanded.

'Good temper,' Elizabeth ticked off the items on her fingers. 'Patience. Now you've got out of the way of being shy and confused when anyone new talks to you, you've a very interesting line in conversation, you know.'

'And a face like a full moon, eyebrows and lashes which look as though they aren't even there, and eyes the colour of nothing at all!' Joan ended disconsolately. 'Isobel'll take one look at me and throw up her hands in the silly, affected way she has and say something like "*C'est impossible*" in that mock French accent she has which we all know she learned at evening classes! No, thanks all the same, love, but I know when I'm beaten. Tim'd have fallen for me long ago if he'd been going to. He's like all the rest. Take Joan out! She's jolly good company. Always game for a lark and a laugh! If only he and the rest of them knew! There's a great deal more to that song "Laugh, clown, laugh" than anyone but a "clown" realises!'

Elizabeth was shocked. As well as she knew Joan she hadn't really realised just how the other girl felt about her own seeming lack of attractions, and yet, Elizabeth thought, appraising her, they were there right enough if she'd only take the trouble to do something with them. Impulsively she pulled out a notepad and scribbled busily.

'Pop along, anyhow,' she advised, 'and take this with you. It's only a few suggestions. Isobel has a "thing" about me for some reason or another, and if she thinks my ideas are OK then you've nothing more to worry about except the spending of a few pounds more than you'd expected.'

'I'll give it a try, anyhow.' Joan pocketed the note and rose. 'You will be coming along when the dance gets going, won't you?' she insisted.

'I promise,' Elizabeth said solemnly, and Joan was content. She had never known the other girl to break her word.

When Joan returned she was transformed. The thick hair had been treated with a special shampoo and lights gleamed in it which neither of them had even suspected were there.

'I'll starve to death before Saturday,' Joan moaned, handing Elizabeth the diet Isobel had written out for her. 'But I'll give it a try. I promised I would and I will, and she says she can promise I won't really be hungry, I might just *think* I am, which sounds more than enough for me! Anyhow, look at my eyes!' she turned her face to the light and opened her eyes to their fullest extent, then blinked rapidly.

'Marvellous!' Elizabeth was sincere. Isobel had used some mascara which she made herself and the effect was to add depth and colour to Joan's grey-green eyes which previously had seemed neither one colour or the other. Elizabeth opened her own almost violet ones in surprise, but she was as thrilled as was Joan by the result.

'You look lovely,' she said truthfully. 'And the dark green dress will just suit you down to the ground now.'

'With this, it might,' Joan reached into her bag and pulled out a length of mock-gold chain. 'It's something she's used in window-dressing,' she explained, 'and she insisted on loaning me some of the ear-rings she uses on the model heads in the window. Look!'

'If this combined effort, plus Dr Roland Bickersley and his hoped-for attentions, doesn't produce the desired effect on Tim O'Toole, then he's not worth bothering about!' Elizabeth pronounced, but she entered with enthusiasm into making certain the diet Isobel had provided was as tempting as she could possibly make it.

On Saturday evening, after duty was finished for the day, a delighted Joan called Elizabeth into the minute bathroom to verify the fact that the scales registered a loss of two pounds.

'And in the right places, too,' Joan beamed in delight. 'I'd never have believed it possible, and do you know? Isobel was right. I haven't really felt hungry at all, even though that diet looked as if a sparrow would have starved away on it, given a full week.'

'Well,' Elizabeth laughed, sharing her friend's delight, 'you haven't had a week, but it certainly seems to have put new life of some sort into you. And you look tons better. Sure you feel OK?'

'Never felt so fit for years,' Joan said fervently. 'And it's done more for my morale than for anything else, and that goes for my figure too. I don't know what it's done to me, but I feel on top of the world. And I like it! I shall stick to this diet as long as Isobel says. She said she'd let me know when it was time to change. Apparently I don't stay on this "starve-me-mother" thing for ever.'

'I suppose it'll be a question now of maintaining her good work, started off by all this,' Elizabeth said gently. 'I told you it wouldn't be so bad once you were accustomed to it! Fruit—of certain kinds—oranges and lemon juice instead of so many cuppas and so on, and you'll soon be as fit as the proverbial fiddle.'

'I'm that now!' Joan boasted. 'I hope we have the Gay Gordons. Last month Tim laughed because it made me breathless. It won't this time. I shall enjoy doing it . . . I used to love dances like that before.'

'I shall hope to be there in time to watch,' Elizabeth said, picking up the small list Miss Lister had written in her cramped writing, all prices carefully noted in the margin of the paper. Any variation, Elizabeth knew, would be equally carefully noted and some minor adjustment made before her next shopping list was ready.

She pulled on her coat and thought about the faded spinster who had the small ground floor flat. It was really part of a larger flat, but the other occupant had no use for all the rooms and willingly let off one room to tiny Miss Lister who lived alone with her two cats, her beloved budgie and her memories as a teacher of 'pianoforte'.

'There's not the same demand nowadays, dear,' she had explained to Elizabeth on the occasion of the girl's first call. 'There was a time, before the war—the last one, you understand—when I had as many pupils as I could deal with, but not any more.'

'I should have thought there was a real interest, underneath all the racket and noise of today,' Elizabeth had started to say, but the old lady had shaken her head.

'Not at all,' she said mournfully. 'Before the first war, and just after, which was when I first started teaching, there was plenty of work. I remember once I had the opportunity of earning a little extra by playing to the silent films, but I was far too busy teaching people's children to play scales and airs from this and that. Two of them—' she mentioned two names each of whom Elizabeth had heard, one as a famous concert pianist and the other in a show group, had started their musical careers with Phyllis Lister.

'They still write to me,' she had confided, 'and they still think I'm all right, you know. I wouldn't have them realise how things have changed since all the television, musical films and what-have-you. A person has to be an exceptional performer nowadays to earn even a modest living at the entertainment game. I was never an exceptional performer,' she had confessed, 'but I think I was a good teacher!'

'You must have been,' Elizabeth said firmly. 'These people would never have made it unless they'd had some good grounding. Let me write and tell them . . .' But she was not even allowed to finish the sentence.

'Certainly not!' had come the immediate response. 'They'd help, both of them, and plenty of the others, I'm sure, but I'm not in such dire need as all *that*, nurse! I have my pension, and the interest from the Bonds my parents left me, and I manage,' but Elizabeth could not fail to notice that each time she went shopping for the old lady the list was shorter, the amounts smaller and the excuse always the same one.

'I don't go out very much, you see,' she would explain quickly when she handed over the list. 'I don't have much exercise, so I don't really need very much.'

Yet the cats and the bird, Elizabeth noted, lacked for nothing, and the only way in which she could help was by buying a little extra for the animals and the bird herself and saying 'this was a free sample' or she had an excess of something she knew the cats would enjoy. Only Bill knew how often she ordered extra milk which went to the room downstairs in order that the old lady should be free to drink the daily pint she ordered for herself *and* the cats!

She shopped and returned with the tiny parcel of groceries, but when she tapped on the door of Miss Lister's room and was bidden to come in, she knew something was missing. It wasn't long before she realised what it was. The radio, so long a companion to the old lady, stood silently in the corner, and it was only after a great deal of coaxing that Elizabeth discovered the set was in need of repair and had been silent for almost a week.

'They charge such a lot nowadays,' the old lady said quietly.

'I know someone who'll repair it for next to nothing,' Elizabeth said blithely. 'He was an out-patient for a time, and I came to know him rather well. It's a hobby of his really, which is why he doesn't make what you'd call a professional charge. May I pop round and ask him to take a look? He only lives in Belle Vue. He could *look* at it without your being under any obligation to him, couldn't he?'

It took quite a time to persuade Miss Lister it would really not be much trouble, and another time to walk round to Steve Wilks in Belle Vue.

Steve was an honest young man, with friendly grey eyes. He had an elderly mother to whom he was devoted, and, as Elizabeth had expected, he responded at once to her story of Miss Lister.

'Tell you what, Nurse,' he confided as he drove Elizabeth back to the flats in his battered old jeep, 'I'll fix it, whatever's wrong with it, for two pounds. Then I'll pretend I've got this old television set on my hands. It's really kept for spares to sets of that kind, but there's nothing wrong with it. I mean, it still works, and gives a fairly decent picture, even though it's small by modern standards. If the old lady likes it she can have it, and I'll tell her about that scheme Mum's joined. She doesn't pay much a week and it covers her for her licence for the TV. Miss Lister could do the same, an' I'll always come in and look at the sets for her if she tells you when there's anything wrong with them.'

Between them they managed to persuade the independent old lady this was not 'another charity offer', as she scornfully phrased it, and by the time Steve had driven Elizabeth back to Belle Vue, picked up the television set and installed it in the small room at Landawne House, the dance had been in full swing for some time. It was comfort enough for Elizabeth to know they had left the old lady enjoying the sight and sound of an orchestral concert, and when Steve had gone, she rushed through her bath and preparations for the dance in record time, conscious of the fact that she had made a promise to Joan, a promise it didn't look as though she would manage to keep!

When she walked into the large hall of the Nurses' Home where the monthly dances were held, it did not take too long to spot the newly alert form of her transformed friend lightly dancing a quickstep with Tim O'Toole. Joan waved as she saw Elizabeth arrive, and when the music stopped she rushed over and took her by the arm.

'Come and sit with us,' she urged, adding in a whisper as Tim went to the refreshment bar, 'Dr Bickersley hasn't arrived yet, though it seems he told Tim nothing would keep him away. Said he felt like treading the light fantastic, especially if Tim'd find him someone worth dancing attendance on as well as with! I'm banking on his coming. You won't let me down, will you?' she urged anxiously.

Smiling, Elizabeth assured she would do nothing of the kind, but almost at once she was claimed as partner by Stan Baxter from the lab, and when he took her back to her seat she was just in time to hear Joan's gasp of sheer astonishment and to turn and see what had happened to account for this phenomenal behaviour. Dr Roland Bickersley had indeed kept his word and attended the dance, but he had brought his own partner. Elizabeth as well as Joan watched in sheer amazement as he escorted the tall, stately form of Ann Lloyd across the room and to a secluded seat in the far corner.

'Well!' Joan's exclamation was quite spontaneous. 'I'd never have believed it unless I'd seen it for myself.

And I do know Dr Lloyd's on duty tonight! What do you make of *that*?'

'Perhaps they've known one another some time.' Elizabeth was always ready to see the other person's side of things and always reluctant to condemn.

'The Lloyds came from up North,' Joan said firmly. 'He told us, if you remember. I happen to know Dr Bickersley has been abroad for some time, some kind of specialised work with unknown bugs or something like that. Anyhow, they seem to be making up for lost time if they did know one another once, and if they didn't they're off to a good start, wouldn't you say?'

Elizabeth said precisely nothing. In fact she was too stunned by the sight of the calm Madonna-like Mrs Lloyd talking with apparent animation and even, after a time, accepting a drink, and later still dancing a modern waltz as though she had been accustomed to doing this sort of thing every night of her life.

For some reason some of the animation of the little group at Elizabeth's table appeared to have evaporated, and although Roland Bickersley came over and chatted for a while his lovely, stately companion remained where she was, alone, and sitting reflectively sipping her drink from time to time and glancing with a cool, appraising stare at the rest of the company.

She acknowledged Elizabeth's friendly wave with a slight, almost indiscernible nod of her head, a fact which caused Joan to give vent to a most unladylike snort of derision and to elicit from Tim a brief not too complimentary remark which Elizabeth instantly quelled.

'Dr Lloyd probably persuaded her to come,' she said, quietly rebuking. 'If he couldn't get away himself perhaps he thought the evening out might do her good, and she certainly looks more alive than I've seen her look, ever since she came to Landawne House!'

Whether it was the heat of the room, the exercise of the dancing or a combination of both—or maybe, as Joan said, simply the excitement of actually getting out of the flat on an occasion which wasn't work—none of them knew. As the evening wore on Mrs Lloyd's colour deepened, her lovely hair loosened a little from the tightly woven coils in which she had piled it, and she looked an altogether different person from the cool, calm and unhappy woman Elizabeth had seen through the partly opened door of the flat.

'Where's your Madonna now?' Joan queried a little maliciously. 'She looks more like the wicked fairy to me. See that sparkle in her eyes? It's visible from here?' and indeed, Elizabeth thought, staring because she couldn't help herself, Mrs Lloyd seemed altogether a different person from the woman who played over and over again the two mournful records which had begun to grate even on Elizabeth's nerves.

'I'll give 'em a lift back to the flat,' Tim offered as the evening drew to a close. 'Might as well. Roland'll be coming back to his room, I suppose, as I'm doing . . .' but he returned from his visit to the others' table with a rueful expression on his sturdy, honest face.

'More or less told me to mind my own business,' he said quietly. 'Seems he's arranged to borrow a car for tonight, and after tomorrow he'll have his own transport, whatever he means by that! Well, it's none of our business, is it? Shall we go, or have you fixed up to leave with someone else, Liz?'

Elizabeth, wary of what she thought of as entanglements, shook her head, but when Tim's badly worn

Austin pulled up at the flats she was out of the car in a jiffy, thanking him over her shoulder and running upstairs ahead of Joan saying she'd put the kettle on, to give Joan and Tim privacy to say a protracted goodnight if they so desired.

It was quite a time before Joan came, yawning, upstairs, a happy Joan with a light in her eyes which Elizabeth had not seen there before.

They had a hot milky drink and were ready for bed, but as Joan drew the curtains after Elizabeth had put off the lights she gave a brief shocked exclamation.

'It's nothing to do with us, I know,' she said before Elizabeth could remonstrate, 'but Dr Bickersley's still out there, in Dr Foily's car, and Mrs Lloyd's with him. I hope someone tells the Doctor! I'd do it myself, but it seems like spying on a neighbour.'

'And if it isn't,' Elizabeth was annoyed, although she could not have said why, 'what else *are* you doing? Come to bed, for goodness' sake, and close the curtains. Thank heavens neither of us is on duty in the morning so it won't matter whether we see light coming in or not! I'm sleepy. Goodnight,' and before Joan could protest or begin a discussion Elizabeth was strangely reluctant to pursue, she closed her eyes and composed her breathing so skilfully that after a moment or so of hesitation as though to make certain the whole thing was genuine, Joan sighed and did as she was told, falling asleep herself almost at once. Yet Elizabeth, eyes closed and ears strained to their uttermost, could have told her friend that a full hour went by before Jack Foily's car drove away and Mrs Lloyd's light footsteps sounded as she ran quietly up to her own flat opposite.

CHAPTER FOUR

THE change in Joan was dramatically obvious. From the night of the May monthly dance she seemed an entirely new person. She did not now require urging to walk the short distance to St Jude's, and Elizabeth, fit as she was, sometimes wondered if she too ought not to take some short physical training course of some description, since it was now she who arrived a little breathless and slightly exhausted after their usually mad rush.

'There's little point in all this "keep fit" lark if it's going to make an invalid out of either one of us!' she grumbled in a friendly fashion. 'I'll have to join in your diet, exercises and what-have-you before long, or else I'll have to start catching the same bus as Mrs Lloyd, then I'll be here to greet you when you arrive.'

She had been joking, but Joan apparently had taken her seriously at her word.

'You're fit enough and slim enough as it is,' she observed, 'but since you were made Sister you seem to have been overdoing things a bit at St Jude's. Matron doesn't expect you to run the place, you know! Sister Murdoch herself said yesterday how changed everything was in Woman's Medical, and how much everyone appreciated the improvement! That's all very well, but there's little point in having an efficient Sister on a ward for a short time, and that same Sister going off sick or something, like having a breakdown . . .'

'I shan't do *that*!' Elizabeth said firmly. 'It's just . . .

oh, I don't know,' she broke off in mid-sentence, which was so unlike the Elizabeth Joan was accustomed to dealing with that she stared in amazement.

'What's wrong, love?' she asked, her tone warm with sympathy, but Elizabeth shook off, with a kind but firm determination, the gentle, comforting hand Joan laid on her arm.

'Nothing, really, I suppose,' she admitted. 'Maybe I need my holiday more than I realised, I don't know. It's just . . .' She broke off again. How could she explain, even to Joan with whom she had shared most of her secrets over the past years of training and nursing, that every time she saw the tall, too-thin form of Dr Michael Lloyd, with his worried expression, his air of not being sure of anything or anyone unless he was at the bedside of a patient, her heart seemed to turn somersaults entirely of its own accord?

'I guess I'm just a little out of sorts,' she managed at last, conscious that Joan was watching her closely and was not in the least deceived by her airy statement. 'I'll ask Dr Walsh or Dr Lloyd for a pick-me-up,' she added, but Joan shook her head.

'They'd both of them tell you to take things more quietly when you're not on the ward,' she said with solemn truth. 'You take on too many worries for other people. And you're such a finickity jinny about the house, what you eat, how it's cooked and all the rest of it. Don't worry so much, love, either about other folks or our own small affairs. None of it's worth it. I always remember an old lady in the first year after training. She said "Remember, lovey, everything passes. It's just a question of sticking things out", and I've proved that's true, over and over again.'

'I'll remember,' Elizabeth promised, and hoped what the old lady, whoever she had been, and Joan were right and that this strange feeling which assailed her every time she caught even a glimpse of Dr Lloyd's figure, hurrying along in his white coat or rushing to the flat, arms crammed with groceries, would eventually vanish.

'I'd better be off,' she sighed, and adjusted her cuffs. 'Sister Worthington said yesterday that it was all very well a Sister living out of the hospital, but it's a great deal more convenient for all concerned if she lives in the Home, and if I'm a second late on today she'll press the point, and I know I'd lose.'

'I don't see why.' The old Joan would have accepted Elizabeth's statement at face value and done all she could to make certain Elizabeth reached Woman's Medical well ahead of Senior Sister Worthington, each morning. The 'new' Joan was disposed to argue!

'I've never known you late on duty yet,' she asserted stoutly, 'and we've been together all the time at Jude's. I should think the only time Sister Mary *could* grumble, with any justification, would be if you ever *were* late. Somehow,' she concluded shrewdly, 'I don't think that's what's bothering you, though, is it?'

Elizabeth smiled and did not answer, but hurrying along to Women's Medical she admitted the truth to herself.

The change in Joan, since the night of the dance, had been marked in no uncertain way, but the change in their neighbour, the taciturn Mrs Lloyd, had been even more dramatic.

To begin with, the two mournful tunes no longer sounded repeatedly, evening after evening. True, she still played the records through once or twice each evening, but not more than that. Even more remarkable was the fact that, although Dr Lloyd seemed to accept every extra duty which could be put upon him, Dr Roland Bickersley appeared to have achieved some sort of working agreement by which someone else always took his turn, leaving him free to spend his leisure as he wished.

'And as what he wishes,' Elizabeth observed to herself as she toured the ward with Night Sister, 'seems to be in any way which will help him to see more and more of Mrs Lloyd . . . and without the watching eye of the doctor to deter them in whatever they're up to . . . which I'm certain bodes no good for Dr Lloyd.'

She had to compel herself to forget Dr Lloyd, Mrs Lloyd and their problems, for Mrs Elliot was being sent home that morning, complete with diet sheet, insulin and instructions. There was some unexpected difficulty, for now, after all her protests at being 'unable to please meself', she did not want to leave Jude's and the care of the nursing staff.

'Can I come back here if things don't go right?' she was demanding fiercely of Nurse Wells as Elizabeth approached. She turned to Elizabeth, as though certain, with her extra rank, she would be able to answer the personal as well as the medical problems which were, or so she thought, now confronting her.

'Dr Meredith's my doctor, Sister,' she explained, 'an' if what I've heard while I've been here's true—and I expect it is—he should have sent me here months ago. Now he says it was me who wouldn't follow instructions! I've followed 'em here, haven't I? Well then! Stands to reason I'll go on following 'em, doesn't it?'

Elizabeth smiled, but kept a certain reserve she felt

sure she needed when discussing a personal matter such as this with so determined an old lady.

'It's for your own benefit to do so, certainly,' she said quietly. 'The problem is, Dr Meredith is a good doctor, but when his patients refuse to follow his advice . . .'

'It didn't seem so important at the time,' Mrs Elliot had the grace to look shamefaced. 'My mother had trouble like this.'

'But medical science was by no means as advanced in those days as it is now,' Elizabeth said firmly. 'There's no point in modern techniques being developed, people giving time and money to research, if people whom their work is intended to benefit refuse to accept the prescribed treatment, now is there?'

'I suppose not,' Mrs Elliot agreed doubtfully, but almost at once she returned to her previous statement: 'That doesn't mean I can't come back here, though, does it, if things go wrong again, Sister?'

'Of course not,' Elizabeth said soothingly, adding: 'I'm pleased to think we have all made such a good impression on you that you would be willing to come back here if you felt the treatment might do you further good! Although,' she continued sternly, 'there's absolutely no reason why you shouldn't continue to treat yourself from now on, in the way you've been shown.'

'Dr Lloyd couldn't come and see me, then?' Mrs Elliot's pale eyes looked searchingly into Elizabeth's own. 'I mean, he only works here, in St Jude's, doesn't he? I know Dr Moore and Dr Somers both come in part-time, I suppose you'd call it,' she continued, naming two of the local GPs who each took on an evening's duty to help combat the short-handedness from which St

Jude's, in common with most of the hospitals in the country, suffered badly.

'I'm afraid not,' Elizabeth said gently, her manner unexpectedly softened by the mention of Dr Lloyd's name. 'He hasn't a private practice in Malenchester, you know.'

'I thought it'd be too much to ask,' the old lady grumbled, 'even though he did say he'd look in on me sometimes to see how I was makin' out. Done me a world of good, has that young man. Better than all the medicine and treatments put together, you might say.'

'If Dr Lloyd said he would look in on you sometime, then I'm very sure he'll keep his word,' Elizabeth said. She was sure, even although she and Michael Lloyd hadn't discussed the matter. It was simply that she felt him to be the kind of person who wouldn't lightheartedly say such a thing to a patient and then let her down almost immediately afterwards.

'If he comes round before I'm gone I'll remind him, shall I, Sister?' the old lady persisted, and as Elizabeth nodded she added: 'If I'm gone before he comes, perhaps you'd remind him for me, will you?'

Elizabeth didn't see how she could possibly bring herself to repeat this conversation to Dr Lloyd, when their only contact seemed to be the businesslike meetings which were part of their daily routine and a brief 'hello' as they encountered one another in the lift or on the stairs at Landawne House, yet she promised, and was rewarded by the look of relief which swept over the wrinkled face looking up at her.

'Bless you both,' Mrs Elliot said solemnly. 'You and Dr Lloyd, Sister. Two of a kind you are, and you'll be rewarded, you see!'

Elizabeth made a suitable comment and passed on to the next bed, but at the back of her mind the little phrase rang repeatedly most of the morning. 'Two of a kind'. Just what had Mrs Elliot meant by that sentence?

'Two suckers, probably,' she told herself, seeking for mental detachment, and instead found herself wondering more and more in what way she and Dr Michael Lloyd might seem 'two of a kind' where their patients were concerned.

The remainder of the day was very busy, almost, Nurse Wells said with feeling, as though they were on a surgical unit! Elizabeth, having had considerably more experience than Second Year Nurse Molly Wells, knew how the girl felt, but as the Ward Sister it was her duty to teach her to take these matters in her stride.

By the time the syncope, a Miss Patterson, had been settled down, given coramine and alcohol, external heat and an electric cradle supplied and oxygen given, Molly Wells appeared to have recovered from her moment of 'flap'.

A Mrs Amberton was another emergency admission, with an aortic aneurysm. Miss Radley, who had been admitted three days earlier as a dry pleurisy, suddenly developed acute symptoms which caused Elizabeth to ask Michael Lloyd to take another look at her when he came up for the second time that morning.

She watched him work, his gentle hands hovering over the woman as tenderly as those of a mother over her first-born. The relief on Miss Radley's plain, lined face was there for all to see, and once more Elizabeth had the feeling that Michael Lloyd belonged in some small town or other where he could hold a well-established practice, where he would be known by everyone, and know everyone, their family backgrounds, their weaknesses and their hidden strengths. It was by no means difficult to realise why Mrs Elliot—and probably a number of the other patients in the ward—looked upon him as a personal friend rather than as the junior medical consultant of a busy and large hospital.

She walked with him from the ward when he had examined Miss Radley and written up the prescription. Although she was listening intently to every word, mentally noting what he said, half her mind was not on the patient at all, but on Michael Lloyd himself.

Despite his air of efficiency—and his undoubted skill as a doctor—there was still, as Joan had said in the beginning, the air of 'a little boy lost' about him unless he was actually beside a patient or writing up the prescriptions.

'It's in himself, somehow,' Elizabeth mused. 'Something in his own inner life that's awry,' and then shut her mind to the memory of Mrs Lloyd and Dr Bickersley sailing off together as they had done the three previous evenings, evidently bent on some form of gaiety. Wherever they went they always seemed to arrive back at Landawne House full of gay spirits, and at all hours of the night. Elizabeth's frown deepened. Dr Lloyd seemed to spend as much time as ever at St Jude's, and what little time he did spend in the flat appeared to be the only times when Mrs Lloyd was either on duty or occupied in the playing—although not so frequently now—of her two mournful recordings.

'No wonder he looks so glum!' Elizabeth thought as she watched him until he turned the corner which led to the children's wards. 'He can't be very happy!'

Whatever his problems were, she reminded herself, it

was none of her business. When he and Mrs Lloyd had
first arrived to take up residence in number five, it had
been quite apparent that all was not well between them,
but it had taken the arrival of Dr Roland Bickersley to
bring some animation to the cheeks and eyes of the aloof
Mrs Lloyd. And, Elizabeth thought sadly, to make the
quiet, attractive Dr Lloyd look more unhappy than ever,
if that were possible, and, to all intents and purposes,
seem to shut him up in St Jude's and out of his own home
with a finality which seemed irrevocable.

Elizabeth might, indeed, have felt it was none of her
business, but it seemed that was not the general idea in
St Jude's. When she went into the day staff's self-service
bar a short time later, she was greeted by Staff Linton
who had worked with her for a time in Casualty.

'I'll get your coffee with mine, shall I, Liz?' she asked,
and not waiting for an answer she pressed the coins in the
machine and was soon seated beside her friend, the two
steaming cups of liquid on the small table before them.

'How you can bear to drink it with only half a spoon of
sugar I'll never know,' Carol Linton made a grimace. 'I
couldn't do it, not even to look like a wand!'

'I just prefer it this way,' Elizabeth said truthfully. 'As
a matter of fact there was a time when I liked it plain
black, and with lemon juice. Excellent in hot weather—
on the rare occasions when we get any!'

'Ugh!' Carol repeated her grimace. 'Not for this child,
thanks! I just couldn't bear that! Might be all right in the
tropics. I understand the new doctor—Bickersley—likes
his that way. Even went to the trouble of importing his
own special brand of lemon juice into the Canteen, or so
they tell me. What do *you* think of him, Liz? He seems a

nice enough chap, but somehow . . .' Her words trailed off into silence and she stared hard at Elizabeth, who didn't seem in the least disposed to reopen the conversation.

Elizabeth finished her coffee quickly and rose. She knew Carol loved to gossip, and she and Mary, the oldest established ward maid in St Jude's, spent many a happy half hour discussing other members of staff and their personal affairs.

The private lives of her fellow nurses and the doctors on the staff held no interest for Elizabeth, or at least, she mentally corrected herself, as a rule they held no interest. Only to herself would she admit that at present she was *very* interested in the private life of one member of staff, namely that of Dr Michael Lloyd. So far as Mrs Lloyd was concerned she wasn't in the least interested, she told herself, so long as whatever she was doing didn't contribute to the unhappiness she was certain the doctor was enduring.

'I know you'll not have a great deal to do with him on duty, Liz.' Carol wasn't going to let the subject drop, it appeared. 'You're on a medical ward, I know, and Dr Bickersley's in Mr Scott's team, like Tim O'Toole. All the same, according to the grapevine, our new friend seems to spend a great deal of his free time in and around a certain flat not very far from yours. A flat, I might add, someone told me you'd been instrumental in getting for him! Would you have helped if you'd had any idea of what would be going on, Liz?' Carol pressed.

'I don't know that anything *is* "going on", as you put it,' Elizabeth said firmly. 'I know Dr Lloyd spends a great deal of time at Jude's and that Mrs Lloyd must be lonely when he's away so much. It stands to reason that if they are friends, he won't mind Dr Bickersley taking Mrs Lloyd around a little. Must give her an awfully cooped-up feeling, alone in the flat, night after night, with no one to talk to.'

'It's funny how often he volunteers for extra duty,' Carol mused aloud. 'Just as it's funny how Dr Bickersley usually manages to find someone to stand in for him! Makes a body think, don't it?' she said jokingly, but it was not a joke to Elizabeth.

'Why people always have to see something wrong in the smallest and simplest of actions, I just don't know,' she said quickly, and the tone of her voice was enough to tell Carol that for some reason or another she had, unwittingly, trodden on dangerous ground. Her interest quickened, and her eyes gleamed.

'You think it's a simple thing, then, that Mrs Lloyd and Dr Bickersley were at the cinema together on Monday, the concert on Tuesday and the Candlelight Dance on Wednesday, do you?' she asked a little maliciously. 'And Dr Lloyd working here each night, until he looks almost fit to drop! He's not content with his own work—as if there isn't enough of *that*—he has to undertake some research into diseases of the bloodstream, along with young Baxter from the path lab. Seems to me the poor chap either daren't, or doesn't want to go home!'

'I don't think you or anyone else in Jude's knows enough about Dr and Mrs Lloyd to discuss their private affairs in this manner,' Elizabeth said stiffly. 'They were strangers to Malenchester when they arrived. What's happened in their lives previous to their arrival here none of us know, I would imagine, and therefore it's none of our business. I'm sure if Dr Lloyd thought there was anything wrong in the friendship between Mrs Lloyd and Dr Bickersley, he's quite capable of sorting matters out to his own satisfaction.'

'Phew!' Carol's chuckle seemed to Elizabeth somehow sinister. 'Why so disturbed all of a sudden, Liz? I've never known you concern yourself about any other man, on the staff or otherwise. What's so special about our quiet Dr Lloyd? He looks as though he's never going to say boo to a goose, but I heard him tearing a strip off one of the housemen yesterday, and I wouldn't have liked to have been in young Maitland's shoes. He's not so downtrodden and meek and mild as he looks, isn't Dr Lloyd! But it seems to me you probably know all about that and a great deal more besides!'

'I don't know anything at all about either Dr *or* Mrs Lloyd,' Elizabeth's quiet, almost reproving tones were in complete contrast to Carol's shrill, near accusing ones. 'I only know they're our neighbours in Landawne House, and that they're about the quietest tenants in the place!' Deliberately she shut her mind to the memory of the everlasting record player, reminding herself that nowadays—ever since the advent of Dr Bickersley, in fact—the record player too had mainly been silent.

'What they do, where they go and with whom, is no concern of mine!' she said coolly. 'Personally I don't think it's the business of anyone else at all except the two people concerned, Dr and Mrs Lloyd.'

'Then there's no point in your getting shirty about it, is there, Liz?' Carol retorted. 'Mary seems to think . . .'

'What Mary *thinks* and what she *knows* appear to be two very different matters!' Elizabeth announced, wishing Mary would remember to pay complete attention to her work on the wards and not concern herself so much with the private affairs of the nursing and medical staff of Jude's. It was a vain wish, as she realised. Mary had been almost what Matron half-smilingly termed 'part of the furnishings' at St Jude's almost since she had left school.

'She said once she'd seen one Matron go and this one come, and that she'd probably last her out as well, and that nursing and medical staff changed so often there wasn't any keeping count, but it was all very interesting. I suppose she's right, and I suppose too there's little else *to* interest her. All the same, I'll have a word with her when I see her again. As well as that I'll do my best to put a stop to all this grapevine gossip! It can't be very good for Dr Lloyd's peace of mind, if nothing else. And he seems so anxious to help, to please everyone . . . it isn't right he should be bothered like this.'

The resolve was firm enough, and indeed she did happen to overhear a snatch of conversation between two of her nurses in the sluice room. The mention of Dr Lloyd's name made her stop short and listen more intently, but whatever had been said was already said, and all she could do was to issue a reprimand about gossip and to leave it at that. Her nurses knew, as did everyone else in Jude's, of her own avoidance of anything which amounted to minding other people's affairs, and after that, at least on her ward, she heard and saw nothing more which might have caused her to worry on Michael Lloyd's behalf.

The rest of the staff, she knew, continued to talk about the number of times Mrs Lloyd was seen out and about with Dr Bickersley, and there was nothing apparently she could do or say about this.

She wondered just how much Dr Lloyd really cared.

Certainly there was no change in his manner or in himself, no visible change, that was. At times she thought he looked just that shade more worried, just that little more abstracted than previously.

In the ward he was as courteous, as helpful and as popular as ever. Whatever was happening in his private life appeared not to have, so far, affected his life at Jude's.

Elizabeth began to feel people were, as usual, exaggerating the situation, but one evening as she walked home, enjoying the welcome warm air of the new month of June, she reached Landawne House just in time to encounter Mrs Lloyd and Dr Bickersley starting out for an apparent evening of gaiety in the smart saloon car she had heard he had hired for the month.

Michael Lloyd responded to her greeting when he arrived back at the flat much later that evening, but Elizabeth, who had just been to the newspaper seller on the corner, felt there was something a little forced about his determinedly pleasant manner.

From the door of their own flat she watched him walk on to Number Five, fit his key in the latch as though, she thought wryly, he fully expected Mrs Lloyd to be out already.

'And she is,' Elizabeth reflected. 'Not even a greeting or a hot cup of tea, or a meal. He might just as well be living in Jude's for all the care she takes of him!'

A couple of hours or so later she was tapping on Miss Lister's door, because the old lady had found difficulty in changing the channels on her newly acquired second-hand television set and Elizabeth had noticed in the evening paper that there was a concert, with a world-famous pianist, at any moment now.

She found the station, adjusted the reception and settled the old lady comfortably in her favourite chair, with everything within easy reach, if she so desired. Miss Lister was lonely, although she insisted as always that the cats and the bird were company enough, but when she said she would make a cup of tea, Elizabeth knew she couldn't rest easily unless she made one and responded to the invitation to 'join me for a few minutes, please, Nurse.'

Altogether the visit, which she had expected to last no more than a few minutes, took almost an hour, and although she felt her visit and her help had been of some value to Miss Lister, she was quite exhausted as she went wearily back upstairs, the lift having once again assumed another 'won't work' phase, as Joan put it.

She had reached her own landing when the door of Number Five slammed shut and Michael Lloyd came hurrying out. He paused on the top of the stairs, hesitated a moment, then, as if he had decided almost on the spur of the moment, he turned to face her.

'Thanks, Nurse Fletcher,' he said quietly, and as Elizabeth could only stare blankly at him he continued: 'I know there's been a certain amount of . . .' she was certain he had been about to say 'gossip' but hastily amended it to '. . . of speculation about our private lives, I mean mine and Mrs Lloyd's. I haven't been unaware of this, or of the fact that you have kindly . . . how can I best phrase it? . . . done your utmost to prevent this . . . speculation getting out of bounds. I'm more than grateful, Nurse, and I know I speak for Mrs Lloyd as well as for myself.'

'I . . .' Elizabeth was annoyed to feel herself blushing. She had believed she had grown out of that habit years ago, but it seemed she had been wrong. 'It really wasn't anything,' she muttered quietly. 'I don't like to hear people gossiping about other people's affairs. One so seldom knows the story behind the reason for what may seem . . . unusual, don't you think?'

'I know,' he said unexpectedly and with such quiet emphasis Elizabeth felt there was more behind the one word than she could guess. 'All the same, thank you again,' he said, giving her one of his rare, charming smiles which so transformed his face he did not look like the same person. 'By the way,' he halted her as she was about to open her own door, 'it's none of my business, I know, and I'm not even responsible for your health via the hospital, but I thought you had looked a little . . . overtired of late. Not too much for you on that ward, is it, Nurse . . . or more correctly, Sister?'

'Not at all,' Elizabeth denied quickly. 'It's actually nothing at all to do with work,' she said hastily, 'my looking tired, I mean. I've been involved in a little private worry lately, that's all. And even that's all right now,' she concluded with a smile. There was no possible way of letting him know it had been worry about *his* welfare which had kept her awake at nights and listless through the days.

'Good,' he said briefly, smiling again. Automatically Elizabeth noticed how often he seemed to smile when he was talking to her and how infrequent were the smiles on other occasions.

'In that case,' he continued, 'I have a free weekend due to me next weekend. How about an afternoon in the country? You must know of several places around the district where we could spend a pleasant couple of hours, and get someone else to make our tea by way of a change. What do you say?'

The temptation was almost overwhelming. A whole afternoon in his company, for she did not for one moment suspect Mrs Lloyd of wanting to share such a simple delight.

At the thought of Mrs Lloyd it was as though a cold hand had descended and placed icy fingers round her heart. Whatever the state of affairs between Dr and Mrs Lloyd, she could not possibly do anything to further impair what she was almost certain was already a very uncertain relationship.

'I'm sorry,' she said, and he was not to know the genuine regret in her voice was because she knew she must refuse and not because of the mere excuse she was about to make. 'I've already promised to go out with some friends,' she said. It would be easy enough to phone one or two of the other staff and arrange something. People were always asking her to join them in this or that, but Elizabeth preferred her free time alone, either reading or making fantastic cookery experiments.

'Like any old maid,' Joan had teased her more than once.

'I'm sorry too,' Dr Lloyd said now, and there was genuine regret in his tone too, so that for a moment she was tempted to retract her lie and tell the truth. Second thoughts, however, seemed to make it imperative to make the little white lie into the truth instead. She would attend to that the moment she was in her own flat, she resolved.

'If you want to know of some pleasant places around

here,' she managed at last, 'I can let you have details of
some of them, especially where there might be music
. . . or books, I believe you mentioned as being Mrs
Lloyd's interests? There's the parsonage just a few miles
away where Mr Amberlon, the eighteenth-century au-
thor, wrote so many of his books . . .'

'Mrs Lloyd will be . . . otherwise engaged, I believe,'
he said, and there was a new coldness in his voice which
made it seem almost as though some other person—a
stranger—was speaking.

'I'm sorry,' Elizabeth said dully, not sure why she was
apologising, but it seemed the correct thing to do just
then. 'I'll let you have the list, anyway. It might come in
useful some time.'

'Thank you.' The words seemed automatic, and
equally automatically to close the conversation. 'That
would be kind,' he added, and then turned and ran
quickly downstairs.

It wasn't difficult for Elizabeth to find friends who
were going out the next weekend. Joan and Tim
O'Toole, Pat Hogarth and Terry Vale, who were both
on permanent night duty and who therefore worked
from Monday to Thursday each week and had a long
weekend in compensation, were only too happy to add
Elizabeth to their number.

'If Dr Bickersley wasn't so taken up by his escorting
Mrs Lloyd all over the place that would have made the
perfect party!' Joan commented, but Elizabeth shrugged
uncaring shoulders.

'Stan Baxter'd like to come,' she mentioned the young
laboratory assistant diffidently. 'He's been wanting to go
over Melton Hall for a long time. This seems exactly like
the right opportunity, then we can go and look at the

new Wild Life park they've opened. It should be interesting.'

Joan continued to make plans for the weekend, knowing that Stan Baxter, exactly like Elizabath, usually spent all his free time with his nose in a book, as Joan phrased it. That could take care of itself when the time came, she thought with a philosophy which seemed to have grown with the 'new' Joan.

Elizabeth was content to let her friend make all the arrangements, but when a picnic luncheon was suggested she did insist she did the cooking.

'I'll make all the things we can pack in foil or vacuum flasks, if you like,' she suggested, 'then we can have a hot or a cold meal, just whichever you prefer. How's that?'

'Fine.' Joan had some experience of the type of food Elizabeth packed, and it suited her to leave the arrangements in her hands. 'I'll fix who's going and in which cars and the route I'll work out with Tim,' she planned. 'We could go on to the Golden Slipper when we get home. They have a cabaret on Saturday nights.'

'I don't think . . .' Elizabeth began, but Joan merely laughed, and Elizabeth said nothing more. It was much easier to let Joan have her own way. She usually did in the long run, anyway.

Saturday morning dawned bright, clear and warm. One small dull cloud in the distance seemed to threaten the brightness of the day, but as Tim had confidently foretold, it seemed to disperse with the first breeze of the midday hour.

They were a happy crowd as they crammed themselves into Tim's old Austin. It was a little difficult as far as leg room went, or as Joan said, 'we're all a little over-size either one way or the other,' but she said it happily, as she would never have been able to say such a thing before her diet and slimmer form.

They drove to Little Bedding, and enjoyed a guided tour of the old parsonage, then went for a row on the fresh-water lake, crammed, according to the guide-book, with all manner of fresh-water fish.

They had their al fresco meal sitting on the grass beside the lake, where the cool breeze off the water helped make everyone feel fresh and once more full of vitality. After that, Tim suggested they drive to the Wild Life park, opened two summers previously, and full of all the birds and beasts, and, Joan's phrase, 'small furry things' which lived in and around Malenchester.

'So many of these little creatures are dying out,' Tim said as they stood and watched with delight a family of squirrels, high in the trees. 'What with the stuff they put on plants, the chemicals they pour into and on to the ground and into the water, it's a wonder there's any natural wild life left at all.'

'A number of creatures seem to have adapted to the newer ways of life, though,' Pat said quietly. 'Take rabbits . . . one would have thought after all the mass efforts that were made to exterminate them there would never have been another bunny in the country! Yet they're almost as plentiful as they were ten years ago, before all this nonsense was thought of!'

More because he liked to argue than for any other reason, Elizabeth was sure, Terry immediately began to argue that the rabbits were a pest anyway, and that the authorities had done the right thing in attempting to control them. A heated discussion broke out, but Elizabeth wasn't even listening. She was wondering where

Dr Lloyd was this warm, sunny afternoon, and what he was doing with his free weekend.

Strangely enough her mental question was answered without her having to put it into words. As though something of her thoughts had communicated themselves to him, Tim suddenly turned to her.

'Did the Frazers, or whatever their name was, who had flat five before Dr Lloyd, ever find anything to grumble about, Liz?' he asked jokingly, 'I mean—is it badly lit, badly placed or anything like that?' he asked.

'They seemed to like it well enough,' Elizabeth said gravely. 'And it's exactly—or almost exactly—the same as ours. Why?'

'Because it seems to be the most unlived-in flat in Landawne House,' Tim retorted, laughing. 'Mrs Lloyd's never in it, and Dr Lloyd's staying at Jude's. He told young Stan here, just before we set out, that he'd stay and look after their joint cultures, although I personally think it's a bit ridiculous to stay and look after something which, after all, isn't his job, just to be working when he ought to be made to take some free time! Heaven knows, none of us really get enough of it to throw opportunities away like that!'

'He's at the hospital?' Elizabeth asked incredulously. 'Then Mrs Lloyd . . .'

'Isn't moping alone at home, don't worry about *that*!' Tim gave a short, hard laugh which seemed to express his own views on Mrs Lloyd and her mode of living more eloquently than any words could possibly have done.

'She said this morning that she'd made her arrangements for the weekend, thank you, and it appears those don't include Dr Lloyd, although I've no doubt they

include our new friend Roland Bickersley!' he added
fiercely.

'It's none of our business, anyway,' Elizabeth said in a
cool tone, but her heart ached as she thought of nice Dr
Lloyd staying at St Jude's on a lovely day like this, when
he ought to have been out in the sunshine, enjoying the
fresh air and some relaxation along with the rest of them.

No one mentioned the Lloyds any more during the
remainder of the afternoon, and everyone seemed con-
tentedly tired when Tim drove the whole party back to
Landawne House.

'I vote we have a snack meal at Sally's Coffee Bar,' he
suggested, 'and then go on to the Golden Slipper. I'd
like to suggest we ate there as well, but it's a bit pricey
unless one has a consultant's screw.'

'I said I'd go back and relieve Dr Lloyd,' Stan said half
grudgingly, 'so that's what I'd better do. He'll get the
evening off then, anyway, whatever he likes to do with
it.'

'Come into our place first,' Elizabeth suggested, suddenly tired of the whole thing and longing for nothing
more than to put her feet up and read her latest library
book in peace. 'I've stacks of steak in the fridge in Bill's
basement. I'll soon knock up something which, although
it might not be as good as the Golden Slipper's idea of a
full-scale meal, will be more substantial—and a lot more
tasty—than sandwiches at Sally's. It won't take long, if
you'll all help.'

Everyone did help. Elizabeth went down to the basement and discovered Bill just about to start out on one of
his infrequent evenings of enjoyment. Every now and
again he felt a nostalgia for the distant past, and when
the feeling came over him he would lock his door and

hurry off to the Ex-Servicemen's Club in town, to spend the evening talking with those whose experiences matched or were at least similar to his own. Hilda, as Elizabeth soon learned, had 'no time for all that nonsense—we have to remember it's all over now,' she told Bill all too frequently. She had already left for her beloved Bingo, and Bill, grumbling softly to himself, opened up the huge freezer and waited for Elizabeth to take out from her corner just what she needed.

'You know where to find me if you want me, nurse,' Bill looked up again firmly. 'You never know when there might be an emergency, you know, but the telephone number of the club's on the back of the envelope on my door. *You* know—just in case.'

'Thanks, Bill,' Elizabeth preceded him back to her own floor. 'I hope there'll never be an emergency big enough to drag you back on duty! You're like so many other people I know, you just don't seem to know when you've really had enough and ought to relax a little. I'll get in touch with you if it's necessary, I promise,' she concluded as he seemed prepared to argue, and, knowing his moods and ways so well, she had no intention of allowing that to happen.

'Mind, it'd have to be a big emergency to make me call you back,' she joked. Then she went into her own flat and began the sort of work she loved almost as much as her nursing, the preparation of a meal appetising and temptingly adequate for friends who were all dear to her.

In the background music from whatever show was in progress on the television masked the buzz of conversation. Joan, enjoying her new-found popularity along with her newly acquired figure, hair-do, make-up and general poise, was keeping the conversational ball rolling in a perfectly adequate manner.

Stan and Pat were looking through Elizabeth's crowded bookcase, taking out a volume here and there and peeping into the contents with every sign of being perfectly contented. Tim, Joan and Terry were half-watching the television screen, half chatting, and, straining intently, Elizabeth was relieved to hear no mention of the Lloyds and their extraordinary behaviour.

Automatically, as she worked, her thoughts flew back to Dr Lloyd. There must be something terribly wrong with his home life if he really preferred to spend his free time at the hospital and in work which, normally, was no concern of his. What sort of woman could Ann Lloyd be, Elizabeth wondered, that she did not, apparently, care whether or not the doctor came home to a friendly face and a welcoming home-made meal, or to a silent flat and something out of a tin?

'No wonder he never looks happy!' Elizabeth frowned as she seasoned the steak and turned on the grill. 'I'd like to . . . sort of "mother" him for a time! He wouldn't look half so lost and lorn if someone took a little interest in his welfare, I'm certain.'

Aware, suddenly, of the way in which her thoughts, quite without any realised intention of her own, appeared to be trending, she did her best to shut them off and to concentrate on the matter in hand. It was no use.

She was placing the perfectly grilled steak on to a serving dish when Tim remarked, à propos of nothing at all, that he bet Dr Lloyd would like to come home to a welcome like this, and from that moment it seemed to Elizabeth that the joy had gone from the evening.

They had fresh fruit salad to end the meal, and everyone helped in the stacking of the dishes, although Elizabeth protested when Pat offered to wash up if the men dried the dishes and Joan put them away.

Suddenly Elizabeth wanted the flat to herself. She didn't want to go with them to the Golden Slipper—or to anywhere else, for that matter—she wanted them all away, out of the flat and to sit and read in peace.

'Leave everything,' she ordered, just as she was accustomed to ordering her nurses on the ward. 'I'll do it very quickly, once I'm on my own, and it'll be much easier that way. I know where everything goes and all that sort of thing, without so many people having to try to help. Run off, all of you, if you don't mind. I've a headache coming on, and I'd like to rush these through and get to lie down before it really gets going. Must have been too long in the sun, I suppose.'

Joan looked searchingly into her friend's face. She had seen Elizabeth with one of her bad headaches, and the sight had not been cheering. She did not have them very often, but when she did all she wanted, needed, was rest, quiet and a darkened room.

'Leave the dishes, love,' she said quietly. 'I'll do them when I come home. I'm not on in the morning, and neither are you, so you have a good rest and forget all about everything. I'll bring you a cuppa when I come in, unless you're asleep and don't want to be disturbed.'

'If the light's off I'll be asleep,' Elizabeth said, feeling suddenly guilty. She had a headache, that was true, but experience had told her when an aspirin would be sufficient to cope and when it would do nothing at all. Tonight an aspirin would suffice, and once she had the flat to herself, the dishes away and the whole place as neat and tidy as she liked to see it, she could relax with her book and soon feel on top of the world.

But would she? She wondered to herself as, with many admonitions not to tire herself or to overdo things, the meal was enough and you did that all by yourself, along with thanks and goodbyes the party dispersed.

It did not take long to have the flat ship-shape and Bristol fashion, as her uncle would have said, but when once everything was in order and she had picked up the chosen volume she had been longing to read, there didn't seem any attraction left in the printed word.

It wasn't until she heard the reluctant whine of the wonky old lift and the sound of quick, firm footsteps along the corridor outside that she realised just why she hadn't been able to settle down and to concentrate on her book.

Without really being aware of it she waited for the sound of the door to flat five opening with that queer squeak it had given ever since she had come to live here, despite all the efforts Bill and the Frazers had made towards getting rid of the noise.

The squeak didn't come. There was no sound of the door being opened, no click of the light switch, something she knew Dr Lloyd always did despite the fact that the evenings were light and there was really no necessity for the glow of the standard lamp which he seemed to have on perpetually whenever he was at home.

Elizabeth tried to possess her soul in patience, but she knew she was straining every nerve to know exactly what was happening out there in the corridor. She heard him move away, go downstairs, presumably to the basement, and then come all the way back upstairs again, and this time he hadn't used the lift. He ran upstairs as though the mere expulsion of some of his physical energy was necessary to him at that particular moment.

She thought she heard him outside her own door and held her breath, ready to spring to her feet the second the bell sounded, but the bell didn't ring. Instead she thought she heard him moving disconsolately away, and suddenly she knew that was something she could not endure. He might have arrived home to an empty flat, but *she* was at home, and she could make him coffee or tea and some sort of snack meal—there was still some steak in the minute larder which she had intended to take back to the fridge later. She was glad now she had not done so.

She made up her mind impulsively and hurried to the door and opened it before she had time to allow herself any second thoughts or regrets. Michael Lloyd was standing midway between her flat and flat five, staring disconsolately at a jumble of items in his hand. He looked up as he heard her open the door, and smiled.

'I've done a stupid thing, I'm afraid, Sister,' he began. 'I seem to have left my key in the lab, and Ann's not in . . .'

'Perhaps one of our keys might fit?' Elizabeth made the suggestion, although she knew all the locks were different as a safety precaution, but he shook his head.

'They're all Yale keys, and all different,' he reminded her. 'And the caretaker's out. I've just been down to see.'

He looked extremely tired, and there was the same dejected air about him that Joan had commented on when he first arrived at Jude's. Impulse seemed to possess Elizabeth that evening. She opened the door of the flat wide and stood aside for him to enter.

'I'll make some coffee—or tea, which ever you like—and if Bill's not back by then we'll try phoning round where he usually goes and get a second key, he's sure to have one. Come and sit down a while. It won't take long.'

At first she thought he was going to refuse her hospitality, but after a second or so of hesitation he pushed the odds and ends back into his pocket with a rueful smile and accepted her invitation to make himself comfortable.

Elizabeth felt a surge of happiness as she saw him lower his long, lean length into the more comfortable of the easy chairs towards which she propelled him, a surge of happiness it was quite impossible to explain.

'Have you eaten?' she asked with a practical casualness which did not in the least deceive herself. She only hoped he could not sense the wordless prayer she was winging heavenwards, hoping against hope she would have the opportunity to look after him properly.

'I had a cup of tea—if that's what they call it—and a bun at the snack bar at the hospital,' he said with a shy smile. 'But I couldn't put you about like this.'

'It's no trouble,' Elizabeth assured him. 'We've just eaten, a whole gang of us, and the things are still here. How do you like your steak?'

He told her, and seemed to accept from then onwards that she was in complete charge of the situation. She gave him the evening paper and disappeared into the little corner screened off as a kitchen, not talking although willing to answer if he should comment.

The television was off now, and the music of Elizabeth's own small transistor was soft and gentle, a programme of light music to which she had half-consciously been listening. She heard him rustle the paper once or twice, then there was silence except for the hushed music and the faint clatter of her pans and cooking utensils.

She prepared the meal on a tray, setting everything as attractively as possible, not stopping to ask herself why she should be taking all this extra trouble. She dared not ask herself why, and she dared not wonder why she was afraid!

She completed the dish with garnishings, brewed the coffee he had said he would prefer, then pushed aside the screen and picked up the tray, a smile on her lips, a light in her eyes which would have caused Joan to wonder had she been present.

Michael Lloyd lay back in the chair as though moulded to the framework. The newspaper had fallen from his nerveless fingers and was lying in a heap on the floor. His eyes were closed and he was soundly asleep.

He woke as she approached him, tray in hand, and immediately began to apologise.

'I don't know what made me do that!' he said as he accepted the tray and Elizabeth pulled up a small occasional table so that he could place the tray on it and pull it closer beside him. 'I've not been sleeping too well since we came here.'

'And working too hard as well,' Elizabeth said gently. 'You ought to take your free time, Doctor. We all need a break, you know, and somehow you never seem to take yours . . . do you, when none of we normally working people in Jude's don't know about it?'

'Sometimes,' he laughed, and almost immediately sobered again. 'It's difficult,' he said, as though in explanation of a question she had not asked in so many words. 'I like the work there . . . but it's not the same as it was in Boldearne. That's where I come from,' he added the explanation as he saw how mystified she looked.

'In Yorkshire?' Elizabeth asked, not because she really cared, but because she wanted to know something, *anything*, of his background.

'That's right,' he said briefly, his eye lighting up so that she knew his home background meant something more to him than simply a place to hang his hat.

'North Yorkshire, to be precise,' he went on, enthusiasm warming his tone. 'It's a small town on the coast. The river that runs into the sea there gives the place its name. It's as full of history as an egg is full of goodness, and that's saying something. The records of the town—small though it is—go back to the times when the Danes used to sail across the North Sea and invade us . . . and that's a very long time ago.'

'You've lived there all your life, have you, Doctor?' Elizabeth wanted to keep him talking, to listen to his voice, watch the play of the various emotions as they sped, one after the other, over his face.

'Yes,' he said more slowly. 'My father and his father and his father before him were the doctors of the town. In fact, Greystones, that's our house, isn't known by that name anywhere. Even the letters from our friends often arrive simply "The Doctor's House, Boldearne," and they find us. Everyone knows us for miles around. It's not . . . not the same, coming to a place where one knows no one and no one knows us or even of us. Perhaps it's as well in some ways,' he said reflectively as though speaking more to himself than to Elizabeth.

She waited a moment, but as he didn't appear to have

anything more to say she asked a question.

'What made you come, then?' she queried, refilling his cup. 'Did you want a change?'

'Ann wanted to come where no one had heard of the Lloyds . . . *our* branch of the family, anyhow,' he said quietly, and to her surprise there was no bitterness in his voice. When he continued speaking it was even more quietly, and she had to strain her ears to hear each word.

'She said she wanted to come to somewhere where she didn't know anyone and no one knew her,' he stated flatly. 'This was the best I could manage, at the time.'

'And you'll . . . stay?' Elizabeth felt it mattered very much just what he said in answer, but what he did say was sufficiently startling as to make her almost wish she hadn't asked the question.

'Just as long as it suits Ann,' he said simply. 'It hasn't been easy for her, and when she's ready for a move . . . then we'll go, not before. I told the Committee all about that when I accepted the position.'

Elizabeth made no comment. She thought of stern-looking Alderman Weeks, Chairman of the Hospital Management Committee, and Mr Kelly, Mrs Webster and some of the other influential people who composed the body of the Committee, and wondered just what magic Ann Lloyd possessed in order to gain such concessions from the people Elizabeth would have felt would have demanded, like Shylock, their pound of flesh to the last drop of blood.

'They accepted you on those terms?' she asked incredulously.

He smiled, pushing his plate to one side of the tray.

'That was marvellous,' he said, 'thank you very much. I've a feeling you've almost saved my life! You were saying . . . oh, yes, they accepted my terms, as you see. Otherwise we shouldn't be here, should we? But I think she's almost ready to . . . move on,' he still seemed to be speaking more to himself than to Elizabeth. 'We must wait and see, but,' he sighed, 'I know it's not been easy for her, but it isn't easy for Dad right now. He's managing the practice almost single-handed, just has someone in from an outlying district for two days of each week. With that and the Cottage Hospital it's more than enough for a man of his years.'

'And you'd like to go back?' Elizabeth felt awful, probing in this fashion, but there seemed no other way to find out anything more about him. He wasn't going to talk, apparently. Anything she wanted to know she would have to dig out of him, word by word, and it wasn't easy since he apparently assumed she knew something of their background, his and Mrs Lloyd's.

'Of course I'd like to go back,' he said as though there could be no possible doubt in the matter and, Elizabeth thought wryly, as though he had expected her to understand that anyway. 'Who wouldn't?' he demanded. 'It's what I've worked for, waited for, all my adult life, but I must remember Bobby, and that it's been far harder for Ann than for me or for Dad.'

Elizabeth, wondering who on earth Bobby was, murmured in a quietly sympathetic manner and hoped he would go on talking, giving her some clue as to what he was thinking.

'It's a fortunate thing Bobby didn't look like me in any way,' he said slowly. 'He took after the other side of the family. I don't think she could have stood being here, even, with me if we'd resembled one another in the slightest.'

'Queer,' Elizabeth thought. 'Bobby must have been their son . . . yet he doesn't appear to be in the least like a bereft father! I wonder if he didn't like the child . . . or was jealous of him?' but looking at the fine, sensitive features, the warm, generous mouth, she knew that wasn't the case. Michael Lloyd could never be the jealous type of man who made his own life and that of those dear to him miserable because of his own jealousy.

'The boy must have . . . met with some tragic accident, maybe died, even,' she told herself. 'That's why he lets her have so much of her own way. But if she ever loved him . . .'

Her thoughts refused to go any further. The thought of Michael Lloyd and Ann being in love, of their living together and having a child—the unknown Bobby—and in some strange way their being parted because of that child, was hateful to her. They *were* parted, she was certain of that. True, they shared a flat, after a fashion; true, they worked in the same hospital, lived their lives, outwardly—as any normal couple. Yet Michael Lloyd was always alone, usually at work. He put in far more hours than anyone else on the staff at Jude's and Ann worked too, but not anywhere where she might come into contact with him during working hours. Unfairly Elizabeth began to wonder if this was what Ann had hoped for when she had applied to work in the hospital herself.

He appeared to be making an effort to pull himself out of whatever unhappy past had him in its grip. He rose and stretched, smothering a yawn.

'I must do something about my key,' he said ruefully. 'I suppose I'd better go back to the hospital and pick it up from there. What a stupid thing to have done! If you hadn't been around I expect I'd have had to go back there anyway, so I might as well do that. I can always snatch a few hours in bed, unless someone wants help during the night.'

'You were on call last night and the night before,' Elizabeth reminded him, and hoped he wouldn't wonder just how she came to know so much about his working life. 'You need your rest. I've just remembered Bill goes to the Ex-Servicemen's Club on a Saturday sometimes. Let's give him a ring there and see if he has a master key and if it'll be long before he's home.'

'It doesn't seem fair,' Michael began to object, then, like a small boy, he confessed: 'But I must admit I'd like to get to bed, and Ann won't be in for hours yet, I don't think . . .'

Judging by the sound of the returning car, for which she'd lain awake night after night when she had known Ann Lloyd and Roland Bickersley were out together, Elizabeth didn't think it likely either. More often than not on such occasions, it was long after midnight when the car stopped outside the flats. After that there was always a long wait, presumably while they talked in the car, before she heard Ann running upstairs, since to use the noisy lift in the small hours of the morning would, as everyone in the place knew, call down Bill's wrath on the head of the offender!

'You sit back and relax,' she advised. 'I'll phone Bill at the club, then I'll make some fresh coffee and we'll chat until he comes if you like,' she concluded shyly.

'That would be fine,' Michael agreed. 'It seems years since I talked to anyone about anything except to do with the past . . .' his voice had deepened as though with some outraged emotion, 'or with St Jude's. Just one thing,' he stipulated, his eyes twinkling. 'promise you'll talk about anything and everything except private worries and the hospital?'

'I promise,' Elizabeth said gladly, and hurried to dial the Ex-Servicemen's Club before starting to make more coffee.

Bill had been enjoying a game of cards, but he said it would not be long before this particular game was ended and then he would, he promised, come immediately. Elizabeth found herself hoping the game would go on for at least another hour, then she happily set to work to make the fresh coffee and to pop into the oven a batch of what she laughingly called 'my instant buns'.

This was a mixture, taught to her years ago, by her grandmother. She always kept some in an airtight tin in the cupboard, then, with the addition of a little baking powder, another egg and a quick beating up of the mixture, the buns were ready to pop into the oven.

They were happily eating, drinking the fresh coffee and discussing the merits of a countryside holiday as opposed to one beside the sea, when someone pounded heavily up the stairs, disdaining the lift.

Elizabeth knew she ought not to have been surprised to see Joan return before her own outing was concluded. Joan, where Elizabeth was concerned, was most attentive on the rare occasions when her flat-mate and friend was under the weather.

'You're like an old hen with one chick,' Elizabeth had laughed at her once, a year or so ago when a migraine, to which she was a victim, had laid her low.

'Nothing of the kind!' Joan had scoffed. 'It's really a case of self-preservation! I can't manage my life without you—or someone like you, to help a bit. That's why when, if ever, I find me a man-friend who'll want to stick to me and to whom I'll want to stick if you follow, I want to be sure he meets with your approval. Otherwise he's out!'

Tim O'Toole did indeed meet with Elizabeth's approval, and no one was more delighted than she that, since the 'new' Joan had emerged, Tim's attentions had increased and Joan's happiness had apparently increased also.

'You needn't have broken off your evening,' she said now as Joan, after a first start of surprise, greeted Dr Lloyd. 'As you see, my headache's gone, and I'm in perfectly good hands if it hadn't.'

'What's this about a headache?' Michael asked immediately, and when Joan explained he wrote rapidly on the prescription pad he carried in his pocket.

'There's an all-night chemist further down Malenchester,' he said briskly. 'If you'll stay with Nurse Fletcher,' he glanced at Joan, 'I'll pop down and have this made up. You could keep it by you for the next time you're threatened by an attack. In any case,' he wrote on the prescription again, 'you'll always be able to get it from him, although it's my belief there's no cure for migraine as such, and won't be until we have a cure for the nervous tension which causes it in the first place.'

'Tim'll go.' Joan pounced on the slip of paper and rushed to the door. 'He'd looked in on Miss Lister on the way back to Jude's. Seems he promised her some records, and he had them in the back of the car. If I had known there was someone in with Liz I wouldn't have hurried, but Tim's going back on duty, so it really doesn't make much difference and I rather think Pat and Terry wanted to be alone for a little while.'

'Dr Lloyd forgot his key,' Elizabeth said with a quiet

note of disapproval. 'I heard him outside and asked him in, and I've phoned Bill. He won't be long, and he can let Dr Lloyd in with his master-key.'

'I'm always forgetting things like that,' he confessed. 'I've been locked out before. My own fault, because, as I've just said, I'm not good at remembering I need a key! I never needed one at home in Boldearne. The doctor's house is never locked up there.'

'Didn't you contact Bill?' Joan asked curiously. 'He's generally around, and if he isn't at home—which would be most unusual—Hilda's there.'

'She frightens me!' Dr Lloyd confessed with such a youthful rougish look that both girls began to laugh. 'It's true,' he insisted. 'She looks exactly like a housekeeper my mother had when we were all children, and nobody, not even mother, dared to defy Emma if she said what she wanted or did not wish to be allowed! I've been in awe of that kind of female ever since—except when they're a patient, of course!'

'I know what you mean.' Joan picked up the prescription which she had let fall on to the table. 'I'll nip down with this, Tim'll bring it back, it won't make him late, and then I'll have some of your freshly baked buns, Liz. Diet or no, you know I can't resist those!'

She was gone in a flash, but the easy intimate moment had gone when she entered, and nothing, it seemed to Elizabeth, feeling abruptly as forlorn as Dr Lloyd normally looked, would restore it to her.

She was wrong, most unexpectedly wrong. She had not, she remembered, bargained for the change in Joan, a change in looks, personality and, apparently, in the very essence of being Joan, which Elizabeth realised she had helped to bring about.

Unlike the Joan of past days, the 'new' Joan set to work to keep up a remarkable flow of conversation which didn't even pause in its torrent when Tim O'Toole returned, a few minutes later, with the tablets Michael had prescribed.

Joan went out to see Tim off, but Elizabeth was still conscious of the fact that the easy atmosphere was gone, evidently beyond recall.

She felt speechless when, seconds later, Joan bounced back into the flat and opened the conversation by saying how stupid it was, when they were such close neighbours and, she felt, friends, to be so formal.

'Out of duty hours I'm Joan,' she announced, 'and she,' she waved an expansive hand in Elizabeth's direction, 'is Elizabeth. We all call her Liz at times, but I don't think she really likes that.'

'Quite rightly too,' Michael's eyes were twinkling. 'I don't approve either. She looks an Elizabeth, and an Elizabeth she'll be as far as I'm concerned, to the end of time. I, by the way, am Michael. Full title Michael Arthur Lloyd Junior. I think it's wrong to be so formal off duty too. Thanks . . . Joan!'

They sat companionably, chatting of their forthcoming holidays. Elizabeth's had been put to a later date in the year because first Nurse Wyburn's appendicetomy, then Sister Worthington's contacting of a virus, had increased work on the wards—for the Sisters under her and the nurses under them—considerably. Elizabeth had now given up all idea of a trip to Norway, at least for this year, but she listened with interest as Michael told them of a mini-cruise he and Bobby had once enjoyed together.

After the mention of Bobby's name, Elizabeth ceased

to listen very much. She was no nearer to knowing who Bobby was, except that he had been very dear to Michael, but that Michael, for some reason best known to himself, did not wear his heart on his sleeve.

She heard Joan talking animatedly about the package holiday she and Elizabeth had enjoyed two years previously, and all the time half her mind was crying out to the other girl to stop her skilful probing of Michael's life.

Not that all Joan's guarded questions were gaining any answers. Michael, it appeared, must have learned in a hard school how to avoid answering what he must feel was best avoided. If she hadn't been so concerned on his behalf, Elizabeth felt she would have laughed aloud at Joan's ill-concealed dismay when all her gentle probing failed to leave her any the wiser than Elizabeth herself.

'Then you haven't travelled very much, Michael?' she was asking now, and was rewarded by a decided shake of his head.

'Not me,' he said firmly. 'We all felt there were enough members of the family trotting around the globe with Bobby and Ann. Mother would never have felt at ease if anyone else had joined in that sort of thing.'

He made 'that sort of thing' sound something out-of-the-ordinary, so that it could not have been simply pleasure which had taken the unknown Bobby and Ann Lloyd a-travelling to wherever they had gone.

'I'm the stay-at-home type,' Michael was saying now, giving his slow, attractive smile. 'I love Boldearne, and I love my own country and its people far too much to want to go dashing off hither and thither, all over the place.'

'Some people are made one way, some another,' was all the comment Joan could make in reply, but Elizabeth, rising to adjust the position of her reading lamp, was sure she saw utter bewilderment in the other girl's face.

'I'm not surprised,' she reflected. 'There's some mystery here, so much is obvious! I should imagine there's a tragic story somewhere in the background, which might explain a great deal. Maybe Ann took Bobby on some sort of trip and there was an accident. Perhaps he finds it hard to forgive her, though he seems to have recovered in himself from whatever the tragedy was! *She* can't forget. That's only likely, I suppose, because, rightly or wrongly, she must blame herself, and I read somewhere once that someone, I'm sure it was Mark Twain, said *"the master passion is the hunger for self-approval,"* and if she can't approve of herself and whatever she's done, no wonder she's such an unhappy person!'

She was still thinking along those lines as the conversation between the other two—if a case of question and answer *could* be called a conversation—finally lapsed, and all three of them were relieved when Bill's voice sounded just outside the door.

'I've brought the master-key, Sister,' he spoke to Elizabeth who had answered his knock, obviously proud of the fact that this time he had remembered her new title. 'You ought to have given me a ring earlier.'

'I wasn't going out, Bill,' Elizabeth said quietly. 'Dr Lloyd's been resting, and that was what he decided he needed most of all. Right now, though, he'd like to get to bed,' she smiled at Michael over her shoulder. 'I'm sure you understand!'

'I'd have a couple of duplicate keys cut if I was you, Doctor,' Bill announced, opening the door to Number Five. 'You an' Mrs Lloyd both being out so much, and not always working the same hours, it might be a help . . .'

'Thanks for the suggestion,' Michael's face was once more sad and resigned as if, Elizabeth decided, he hadn't needed reminding that he and Mrs Lloyd were seldom in—or out at the same place—together. 'If we decide on that and I let you know, perhaps you'd arrange to have it done for me? I wouldn't know where to find anyone to do a job like this in Malenchester.'

'Frank Swinden,' Bill said without hesitation. 'Just say the word, Doctor, and I'll see about it whenever you wish.'

Michael made some appropriate murmur of thanks and retired into his own flat, closing the door gently behind him. Bill stayed on, chatting for a few minutes longer, but Joan was eager to learn how Dr Lloyd had come to be their guest, even for a few hours, and Bill found himself unceremoniously cut short and Elizabeth, hustled before the suddenly animated figure of her flat-mate, was soon inside her own domain.

CHAPTER FIVE

'How did all that come about?' Joan demanded as soon as the door was closed. 'Did he come knocking on the door and asking for company, or what?'

'I've told you once,' Elizabeth said a trifle wearily. 'He just forgot his key, and I thought he looked so tired he'd be better in here with a cup of coffee than walking all the way back to Jude's when he'd done an extra stint into the bargain.'

'It's obviously his own fault, and I expect he prefers things as they are,' Joan said ruminatively, 'but it's a funny situation as I see it. He's one of the nicest and most attractive men I've ever encountered, and yet she seems to go to any lengths to avoid either being in the flat with him, or going out with him when he's not on duty. If that's the way things are, it seems to me they'd be better properly apart, then they can each make a new life for themselves instead of living this no-life-at-all kind of existence. He could live in at Jude's if he cared to, and he'd certainly not be called on much more than he is at present! Seems to me he likes being available to his patients, but maybe not to Mrs Lloyd.'

'I don't think that's it.' Elizabeth could have bitten back the quick denial the moment the words were uttered, but it was too late. Joan pounced on them at once.

'Then what is it?' she demanded, 'and how do you know things aren't the way they look, both to me and to

117

everyone else at Jude's? They'd look like that to you too, if you weren't so head-in-the-air where all men are concerned. I saw him looking at you tonight when we were talking. I bet if she were out of the way you'd be out and about with our Michael pronto, if he had anything to do with it. And to judge by your own expression, every time you see him, I don't think you'd mind, would you?'

'I haven't thought about it.' Elizabeth knew she was not speaking the truth, and she knew Joan had realised that too, but even so, she would not face up to the truth within herself, let alone discuss it with someone else.

'Poppycock!' Joan said scornfully. 'You know you have, and you know he has too! It's the first time I've seen you even change colour when anyone's taken notice of you, and heaven knows there have been plenty of staff at Jude's would have given a great deal to take you out, even before you got to Staff.'

'Water under the bridge,' Elizabeth said reprovingly. 'You know I'm set on my own career. That's more important than any good time you and Pat and the others seem to think is so wonderful. I like a bit of fun, an outing, a dance, all the rest of it. But I'm not in the least interested in attaching myself to one male. Not yet for a long time, anyhow. And it's my private opinion there's some real and perhaps tragic reason for the peculiar way they live. Listen.'

Joan listened in almost complete silence as Elizabeth retold most of the conversation she had held with Michael. She didn't retell everything. Not the way in which he'd thanked her for all her help, or the fact that he'd said they would only be staying at St Jude's 'so long as it suited Ann'. That, somehow, seemed a private sort of remark he had made to her, and she could not bring herself to believe he would have talked so freely with anyone—not even Joan—present.

'It certainly does sound very fishy, to say the least,' Joan said frankly. 'It couldn't have been anything he'd done wrong, or he'd have been struck off. Seems you could well be right and whatever it was that happened was some sort of a tragedy and most likely her fault. She looks as though she carries some sort of weighty secret, and you may be quite right in assuming that's why they live as they do. Yet,' she went on passionately, 'it isn't fair—whatever the reason—for Dr Lloyd to have to live this way too! I'm sure he's the sort of man who'd be most content as a GP in some comfortable but busy area, somewhere where he knew everyone and everyone knew him.'

Elizabeth was startled by the other's perception. She had not mentioned how nostalgically he had spoken of Boldearne, simply that he had said his people, for generations before him, had been the doctors of their home area, and that he would have liked to carry on . . . and to save his father work.

'I should agree with that,' she said simply, yawning as she began to prepare for bed. 'I'm for turning in. I'd like a really long lie-in in the morning, then think of something not too energetic for the afternoon . . . but duty will call in the morning.'

'Mrs Lloyd hasn't come in yet,' Joan said casually, as though Elizabeth had not spoken. 'I wonder where she goes and what she and Dr Bickersley find to talk about so much? Whenever you see them together they're both talking away nineteen to the dozen, just as though they had an awful lot to say, to arrange, and little time in which to do it, whatever it is. I'd feel a great deal happier about Michael Lloyd if I knew just what Mrs Lloyd's up to.'

'It's none of our business, anyway,' Elizabeth said firmly. Joan, she felt sure, would realise she was really telling that to assure herself that the way in which the Lloyds led their lives was entirely their own concern.

'I suppose not,' Joan assented cheerfully enough, 'but you must admit it's intriguing! And annoying. I'm all for a good mystery myself, when it's in a book or on television. I must confess that in real life I find them more annoying than satisfying. And if you're really honest you'd admit as much yourself. Shall I put the kettle on again and make another cuppa?'

'If you'd like one.' Elizabeth knew from past experience just what was in Joan's mind. She had some idea of talking about Michael Lloyd, until, by degrees, she had wormed the whole of their evening's conversation out of her friend. Normally Joan was no more interested in the grapevine gossip than Elizabeth was herself. Yet, every now and again, something interested or intrigued her, and she was like a small, determined terrier in the way in which she persistently held on to whatever small facts she could collect until she had what she believed to be the whole story, clearly embedded in her mind.

'I shan't tell her any more,' Elizabeth resolved, and shrank from any idea that this decision was because she herself wanted to hold on, mentally, to the private conversation she had held with Michael Lloyd before Joan had returned.

Joan made the tea and brought it to Elizabeth with an air of solicitude which was most disarming.

'You've been waiting upon other people all night, Liz,' she said in explanation. 'Now I'm fussing you, by way of a change. I wonder,' she added as though the thought had just occurred to her, 'if Michael has anything to eat in his flat?'

'I made him a meal,' Elizabeth said briefly, and then wished she had not said anything. Already she could see Joan making mental—and in all probability completely wrong—images of herself and Dr Lloyd having an intimate meal for two. Probably, she thought, suddenly angry, Joan was picturing the lights turned down, the radio playing, and herself curled up in her favourite position on the goatskin rug at Michael's feet.

'He fell asleep while I was getting it ready,' she said starkly. 'The poor man seems worn out, and even all the work he's been doing since he came here shouldn't account for such weariness. It's not as though we're in the throes of an epidemic or anything. He's likely one of those people who are never really satisfied until they are working themselves almost to a standstill. Perhaps that's what's wrong. Maybe she's like the rest of us and only wants to put in extra hours when it's absolutely necessary! He seems to live for the hospital and the patients and for nothing else at all.'

'You like him, don't you, Liz?' Joan did not look at her friend as she poured the tea, but Elizabeth could sense she was being watched by reason of her image in the mirror on the wall opposite.

'Of course I like him,' she said a little impatiently. 'There's nothing to *dislike* about him, is there? But that doesn't mean I can't feel a little sorry for her if he's so tied up in his work he hasn't time to take her out, or sit at home and chat one evening a month! Do you realise they've been here just over two months now and the only time we've seen them go out is when they go to work or when she goes out with Dr Bickersley? It can't be much fun for her.'

'She's making her own,' Joan said unrepentantly, 'and that's what I'd like to see him doing. You *do* like him, don't you?' she persisted.

'I've said so . . .'

'Then, if Tim asks him out with Pat and Stan and Tim and myself, will you complete the party?' Joan queried. 'We'll know when Mrs Lloyd and Dr Bickersley are going out again, because Tim gets the wire from Dr Ford. Seems Bickersley keeps enquiring about new places to take "his friend", and we all know who *that* is!'

'No, no, thank you.' Elizabeth drained her cup and rose, making a determined effort this time to get to bed. 'Count me out, please!' she said firmly. 'Whatever's wrong there is no concern of anyone else but Dr and Mrs Lloyd! I know none of us think he's fair to her, but we don't *know*. There's no way in which we can know, either, unless one of them cares to confide in us, and I somehow don't see that happening.'

'He gave you no clue, no hint?' Joan persisted, and as she saw the impatient frown which began to crease Elizabeth's forehead, she halted abruptly in whatever she had been about to say.

'All right,' she said, half laughing. 'I won't press for any more details. It's just . . . now I'm so happy with Tim, and it's all thanks to you taking an interest in my appearance and what-have-you, I feel I want to see you happy as well! Did I tell you Tim and I are to be married when he's finished here? He's trying for a small share in a group practice in a Midland market town. I'm absolutely thrilled. We're going shopping for an engagement ring next pay-day. We don't have to wait until then, but

Tim's always too ready to draw out any money he has managed to save, and I'm insisting this time he keeps a bank account with something other than an overdraft in it! We've got to do something serious if we're going to get off on the right foot.'

'You will, and . . . congratulations,' Elizabeth moved forward and planted a chaste kiss on Joan's flushed cheek. 'You'll make a fine doctor's wife in a market town,' she teased. 'And you'll be as busy as anyone else, with your coffee mornings, your sales-of-work and all the good deeds which go to the make-up of such a way of life.'

Joan didn't know it, of course, but Elizabeth was thinking of a small seaside town, where 'the doctor's wife' from 'the doctor's house' had shopped, each wife in her turn, for generations. There was something suddenly very appealing in this thought of continuity! Even more appealing, she decided, than in being an aloof and alone person as she had worked for and dreamed of so persistently for so many years.

'I know you'll be happy, Joan,' she said now as they undressed, each in her own section of the flat. 'You're so right for one another.'

'And so will you be, one day, and maybe before long, love,' Joan said with such complete assurance that Elizabeth, ridiculously, was tempted for a moment to believe her. She made no comment, however, and soon afterwards she heard Joan's breathing develop into the light, regular rhythm which told her friend she was asleep, perhaps happily dreaming of her beloved Tim O'Toole.

For her part Elizabeth lay awake until long after she had heard the car bringing Dr Bickersley and Mrs Lloyd back to the flats. The car didn't wait long tonight, or rather, she thought, glancing at the luminous dial of her watch and noting it was well after two o'clock, this morning. Mrs Lloyd didn't use the lift even after midnight, and Elizabeth strained her ears to catch the sound of the light footfalls as she went home.

'I wonder why he was so insistent on two bedrooms?' she asked herself sleepily. 'Things must have been . . . difficult . . . before they came to Malenchester! If only she were more approachable!'

She fell asleep at last, to dream a confused conglomeration of pictures of Dr and Mrs Lloyd on a raft, pushed out to sea, with Dr Bickersley standing on the shore and looking so woebegone that, even in her dreams, Elizabeth felt sorry for him.

After that she dreamed that Michael Lloyd had come to her flat again and said he would have to go away, that he could not stay any longer in the same building as herself, with nothing more than an empty friendship between them.

She woke after the alarm had run itself down and was silent, a fact so strange that Joan (who normally was sufficiently reluctant to drag herself from sleep that she waited until Elizabeth had made the first cup of tea for the day, then she would force herself to get out of bed and stagger along to drink hers) raised herself on one elbow and looked across the intervening space of the bedroom to see what had happened.

As though the intensity of her friend's gaze had managed what the strident alarm had failed to produce, Elizabeth too awoke, stared at the clock for a moment and was instantly out of bed.

'Why didn't you shout?' she asked. 'You must have

heard the clock! That's the first time I've overslept since we left the Home. Come on, Joan, we'll have to hurry.'

It was as well they did hurry. Only the previous evening Elizabeth had remarked, 'It isn't as though we're in the throes of any epidemic or anything.' Once they reached Jude's it was obvious that she must, unwittingly, have experienced some form of premonition.

Throughout the day case after case of acute influenzal gastro-enteritis arrived from one doctor or another. By lunchtime Matron had decided on barrier nursing on Women's Medical, and a special ward had been set up to cope with all cases as they were admitted.

Elizabeth had spent some anxious hours when she had worked on Surgical Unit, but none of them were any worse than this present and totally unexpected epidemic.

'It's that warm, moist weather, and then the sudden change of temperature,' Sister Worthington grumbled as she organised her dripping, disinfected sheets, the special bowls for the extra frequent washing of hands, the masks and gloves Matron insisted upon being worn by everyone who came into contact with the wards where those affected had been taken.

'I can understand this sort of thing in spring, autumn or winter, you know, Sister,' she expostulated to Elizabeth as they organised yet another side ward, this time for the newcomers for whom no beds in the regular wards could be found. 'It's all this whizzing about in space that causes it, I'll be bound. I know people say the weather's never changed, that there have always been summers like this one, and so on, but I don't believe it. When I was a little girl,' she went on, 'we all had new frocks for Whitsun, and after that we put our winter woollies away until after Bonfire Night. Now,' she gave a ladylike snort of derision, 'it's impossible to tell one season from another, and the sort of illnesses we used to get only in the winter are thriving all the year round. So much for progress!'

Elizabeth smiled but did not comment. There was little point in attempting to argue with Rose Worthington when she had made up her mind about anything. Years ago, when the first whisper of the project of a man in space had been seen in the newspapers and on the television, Rose had decided 'no good'll come of it'. Since then, although an extremely sensible woman in almost every other way, nothing would convince her but that all the new illnesses, all the hitherto unexpected but accepted vagaries of the English climate, were the direct result of 'getting above ourselves', as she phrased it.

Elizabeth did not argue. For one thing, there was too much to be done and too few hands to do it all. For another, experience had taught her it would be a complete waste of breath. It would be equally futile to mention all the surgical miracles of the post-war years. Rose was 'interested', but not fully approving, and Elizabeth did not feel disposed to enter into a discussion which she knew would last the remainder of the day.

St Jude's was normally a busy hospital, now it was even more busy than usual. By the end of the day, seeing Michael Lloyd walking along the corridor as she headed for the day staff cloakroom, Elizabeth felt a pang of sympathy for the victims of the epidemic, for she ached from head to foot as though at any moment she too would become a sufferer in any one of the hastily arranged extra wards.

'What a day!' Michael greeted her as they drew level. 'I'm ready for home this time. What about you, Sister?'

'Almost too tired to get there,' Elizabeth smiled, and was rewarded by an answering smile from his sensitive mouth and clear friendly eyes.

'Frank Haslem,' he mentioned the physiotherapist, 'said he'd give me a lift home. He's been working late on Out-Patients. If you don't mind a bit of a squash I'm sure he'd fit you in as well. What about your friend, Nurse Barstow?'

'She's on till eight today,' Elizabeth said, admitting her weariness despite her resolve, 'and if Mr Haslem will be so kind as to fit me in too, I'd be everlastingly grateful.'

'I'll tell him,' Michael said. 'He said he'd pick me up out front in four or five minutes. We'll wait for you.'

Elizabeth had not had a great deal to do with the thickset physiotherapist, but what she had seen of him she had liked very much. Just then, she reflected as she pulled on her coat, it wouldn't have mattered if Frankenstein himself had offered her a lift. She would have accepted equally gratefully, she was so utterly bone-weary.

There was no difficulty in fitting her in. The roomy Rover car, although long since past its better days, was comfortable, and it was a relief to be driven to the actual doors of Landawne House without even the brief walk from the bus stop.

Michael helped her out of the car, although she could have managed quite well unaided. There was something comforting and reassuring about the feel of his hand under her elbow. It gave her the strangest feeling of being protected, cared for . . . *cherished*, she thought over the lovely, old-fashioned word and revelled in its use in her mind. It gave her a comforting glow, a glow which lasted until Frank had driven away and she and Michael stood in the entrance hall of the house.

Mrs Lloyd was just descending the stairs. She looked as cool and as immaculate as ever, and, Elizabeth decided, as inscrutable too. Despite all her recent outings and presumed gaiety, she still had the look of a statue of the Madonna, or a pictured face of an old painting from some mediaeval church.

She paused about three steps from the bottom and looked at them appraisingly.

'I shall be home late, Michael,' was all she said, and as Elizabeth looked at him the sensitive mouth tightened a little and she could have sworn his hand, not the one under her elbow but the left one, clenched almost involuntarily.

'Very well,' was all he said. 'Enjoy yourself!' then he and Elizabeth were ascending the stairs side by side while Ann went coolly out of the door, pulling on a thin pair of gloves as she went.

'What about your meal?' Elizabeth couldn't hold back the simple remark.

'There'll be . . . something,' he shrugged, as though the matter were of little importance. 'There are all sorts of tins and packets in Ann's store cupboard. I'll find something.'

'Do you like omelettes?' Elizabeth asked impulsively. He nodded.

'Then we'll have omelettes,' she decided, 'with mushrooms. I always keep a tin of those little button ones, and there's always masses of eggs. Since Joan went on her diet we seem to have eggs and eggy dishes until it's a wonder we don't both cackle!'

She was talking nonsense, and she knew it, but she couldn't forget that strange look in his eyes when Ann had said so casually that she would be late home.

When was the woman ever early at home? Elizabeth wondered, then checked her thoughts in case she said aloud something she might afterwards regret having said.

Michael, as this was not his first visit, seemed to have the hang of things remarkably well for a man, she decided. Perhaps because he had to do so much for himself it was second nature for him to crack the eggs into the basin, to add the seasoning and begin to beat lightly as Elizabeth set the table.

'I can manage,' she told him repeatedly, but he only smiled.

'Too many cooks may spoil the broth,' he joked, 'but when we're both as tired as we are, then I think it's a case of extra hands helping to make light the work, don't you? Mother never refused help in the kitchen when there was any epidemic scare on, and when I was a boy that happened far more frequently—and far more frighteningly and dangerously—than it does nowadays. Anyway, it's good for a man to know a little about cooking, just as a woman ought to know how to fix a fuse or a tap. There are times when it's necessary, and it's as well to have at least some idea . . . or so we were taught when we were children. I've often found these little things more useful than some of the major tasks set us when we were young.'

'It's the little things that go to make up life, isn't it?' Elizabeth said, carefully measuring the beaten mixture into her omelette pan. For a moment he looked startled, as though such an idea had not occurred to him, then he smiled.

'I suppose that's true,' he said reflectively. 'One doesn't notice how the little things add up until they become the big things, the major things, and then, I suppose, it's too late.'

Elizabeth was startled, but said nothing. The closed, hurt look was back on his face, as though someone had dealt him a severe blow and he didn't know why. Elizabeth felt her heart harden towards the woman they had encountered on the stairs, then her naturally charitable heart reminded her that she knew nothing, really, of their story. She remembered an old French proverb she had learned at school and which ran '*To know all is to forgive all*' . . . and, in common with most of these old sayings, there must be, Elizabeth decided, a certain amount of truth in the words.

She didn't pause to analyse it now, but deliberately, although she was so tired, she made their conversation interesting, intent only on chasing that hurt, puzzled look from his face, and by the time the meal had ended she had the satisfaction of seeing him smile again and lean back in his chair, replete and contented.

Michael seemed content to sit back, smoke a cigarette and relax, listening to the softly playing radio and occasionally making an odd remark about one aspect or another of their separate lives at Jude's.

He stayed with her until it was almost time for Joan to return, and then, as though he didn't want to face any more company that evening, he said he had some notes to write up and left to go to his own empty flat.

Elizabeth remained where she was. She didn't even

get up to move the dishes. She sat, curled up, on the goatskin rug which had been a flat-warming present from her aunt, and stared into space, seeing only Michael Lloyd's face in place of the switched-off fire she was facing.

If only he hadn't looked so . . . hurt . . . and yet, she frowned, that didn't seem to be quite the right word to express what she had felt when she had seen his face as Mrs Lloyd made her announcement.

He had looked more puzzled than anything, she decided. Certainly he didn't look angry or as though he wished she would have stayed at home. He'd been content enough in Elizabeth's flat. She was sure he had enjoyed his spell at the stove, and she was equally sure he had left her feeling refreshed in more ways than by means of a satisfied stomach and the stimulation of fresh coffee.

'He makes me want to take care of him,' she thought, a little shocked by the idea, but the more she examined it the more it appeared to be the truth of the matter.

She thought back over her years at St Jude's. Michael, although to listen to Joan one would never have believed it, was not the first man in her life. There had been Tommy, the gay young journalist who had been admitted with a fractured leg when she had been on Men's Surgical, who had persistently asked her to go out with him from the moment he was allowed to use crutches.

That hadn't lasted long, Elizabeth reflected, smiling to herself. Tommy had been a good friend, a pleasant person to be with, but his mind was like quicksilver, darting here, there and everywhere, and he sought for items of news interest even when he was on sick leave.

Although she had been the one to be fit and well, and

Tommy still a patient, she had been the one to become exhausted after an hour or so in his company. He never seemed to be still, either mentally or physically, for more than a moment, and Elizabeth had found this most wearing on her nerves.

After Tommy, and as though in complete contrast, she had gone around for a time with John Sanders, who acted as Chief Clerk to the Committee, and who was just as much of a recluse as Tommy had been inclined to the gayer side of life.

For some time after John's departure, she had not gone around with anyone special. She had joined in with the rest of her year, attending the monthly dances, going occasionally to the cinema or to a concert, but being careful—although she could not have said why—to form no sort of serious attachment with any one man.

When Andrew Taylor had joined the staff of the laboratory at Jude's she had been attracted by his shy, diffident manner and his general air of being unsure of himself. At first he had accepted her solicitude, her instinctive mothering of someone who seemed quite unable to cope with life by himself. All had gone well, until one night, returning from a visit to an out-of-town Country Club, Andrew had, in Joan's words, taken too much for granted, and after her first feeling of fright and of being in some way let down, Elizabeth had turned completely to her solicitude, her instinctive mothering of someone who would ever mean as much to her as her work did from that moment onwards.

There hadn't been, either, she reflected, until Michael Lloyd had come to Jude's. She stirred uneasily, partly because she was becoming cramped by remaining for too long in the one position and partly because even the thought of Michael seemed to do something to her consciousness.

'Hello, love! Sitting brooding?' Joan had swung open the door and switched on the main light so that Elizabeth, who had been enjoying the fading light of evening, blinked in the sudden brightness.

'*And* you've had a visitor, I see,' Joan eyed the table, smiling. 'Anyone interesting?'

'Just Dr Lloyd,' Elizabeth made herself say his name in a quiet disciplined voice, as though the very act of its utterance didn't set the blood pounding in her veins and her heart beating as though she had been running fast and for a long way.

'Just Dr Lloyd, eh?' Joan grinned happily. 'Just another act of charity on your part, pet, or was there some other reason? He wasn't locked out again, was he?'

'No,' Elizabeth said briefly, then the rest of it came out in a little rush which, although she did not realise it, allowed Joan to guess more of the truth than Elizabeth would have realised was possible.

'I . . . we were both late home,' she said in explanation. 'The medical wards are all full to bursting point, as you know. We were both tired, and Frank Haslem gave us a lift back to the flats. When we arrived Mrs Lloyd was just going out.'

'And?' Joan prompted as she paused.

'And all she had to say was that she'd be home late,' Elizabeth said crisply. 'She didn't even ask if he needed—or wanted—a meal! She doesn't deserve a man like him!' she added with a crisp viciousness which was totally unlike her normal self.

Joan stared at her friend with a speculative air. Happy

with her Tim, she had suddenly become more sensitive
to the moods and imaginings of others.

'You like him a lot, don't you?' she asked casually.
'More than like him, if you tell the truth.'

'How can I?' Elizabeth said scornfully. 'You've forgotten, there's Mrs Lloyd . . .'

'You're old-fashioned,' Joan said in her forthright
manner. 'She doesn't worry about him, and from all I've
seen he doesn't worry *too* much about her! He did his
best to find accommodation for her before they arrived,
and then he's never here—or seldom. When he is, she
isn't. I shouldn't think you have too much to worry about
there, love!'

'I would never dream,' Elizabeth knew she sounded
prim and hated herself for it, but she went on, 'of even
thinking or doing anything which might harm his career,
and you know that any sort of a scandal could and would,
especially in a town like Malenchester.'

'Malenchester's no worse than anywhere else,' Joan
retorted, 'and a lot better than most places. Most of the
folks here are OK too. I shouldn't worry about *that* if I
were you! But I would worry if he thinks he's going to
use you as a convenience, someone to come to when
there's no one else around to look after him! I wish I'd
come home with you and seen her setting off again
without him! I'd give a great deal to tell·that madam just
what I think of her! It would serve her jolly well right if
he decided to run away with the most attractive junior
nurse at Jude's! Or any one of the attractive visitors who
come fussing round the medical staff, thinking they're
going to get special attention for their nearest and
dearest—as if we made any difference between any of
the patients!'

'He'd never do anything like that,' Elizabeth said with conviction. 'And if he did, it's none of our business really. He's just another neighbour.'

'Are you sure that's all he is, Liz?' Joan insisted quietly. 'I don't think that's quite true. Dr Michael Lloyd means a great deal more to you than you'll admit even to yourself! I know you, my love, and to me it's as plain as the nose on your face! I'm going to put the kettle on,' she interrupted herself to add. 'You'll feel a sight more cheerful when we've had a cuppa.'

Elizabeth sat still, a fact which made Joan turn from the door of the small kitchen and look at her with real anxiety. This was not in the least like Elizabeth; in all the years in which they had been friends Joan had never known the other girl sad or despondent; now she sat still as a statue, as though prepared to remain for ever in the one inactive position. As though, Joan thought with sudden clarity, life as she had been living it for the past twenty-odd years had ceased to exist.

Joan made a cheerful clatter in the kitchenette, keeping up a rapid fire of conversation and entirely ignoring the fact that her words were not bringing forth any answer from the girl curled up on the rug.

'Had a couple of interesting cases on Men's Surgical today,' she began, and without waiting for Elizabeth to comment she went on to describe the cases in detail, until she had run to the end of her story.

She did glance round at Elizabeth then, and saw her expectations were justified. The other girl had not been listening to a word and only when Joan's voice had ceased did she rouse herself enough to say quietly: 'I wonder what's made them like this?'

She's thinking of him all the time, and won't admit it,

Joan decided. She knew the feeling so well. For a long time she'd dreamed of Tim O'Toole and how wonderful life could be if he once saw her as a person, not simply as an extra pair of hands in the ward.

That part of her dream, Joan decided, had come true. Tim and she were to be married, and each time they met, whether at work or off duty, it seemed there was still something more to be discussed, something else to be decided, and in which they must both take a part.

'That's part of it,' Joan decided, pouring the tea. 'It's having someone—*the* one—who really cares as you do! Tommy and all the rest didn't mean much to Liz, they were just good fun to be out and about with. Michael Lloyd's the sort of man she'd stick by for ever . . . but there's Mrs Lloyd . . .'

Somewhere on the lower floor there was the sudden sound of commotion. Doors slammed, people were running and someone was calling out in a loud voice, a voice which seemed to be crying for help and at the same time expressing pain, fear and some sort of anger, all mixed up in a combination of sounds.

Elizabeth sprang to her feet and together the girls raced downstairs to where the noises appeared to be coming from . . . the door of Miss Lister's room.

Elizabeth turned the knob and rushed inside, slamming the door quickly behind herself, almost injuring Joan, but that brief glimpse had been enough to see the reason for the hastily closed door *and* for the screams.

Miss Lister, it was obvious, had been making herself a drink. Handicapped as she was by the partial loss of the use of her legs, there were times when she scorned to use the sticks with which she had been provided to help her at least get around her own home in safety.

She had told Elizabeth on one occasion that she used her tiny, old-fashioned spirit stove to save her electricity costs. Somehow Elizabeth had always been secretly afraid of the small, insecure contraption upon which Miss Lister boiled her kettle. Now, it seemed, her fears had not been without some foundation.

It was only afterwards that they learned the full story. Miss Lister had been about to pour the boiling water on the tea to infuse the leaves when she had caught the fork of one of her sticks in one of the loops in the home-made rug of which she was justly proud.

She had fallen heavily against the light stand on which she balanced the little stove. The whole thing had tipped over, flames from the burning spirit snatching with eagerness at the decorative old-fashioned hangings and even at the gauzy scarf which Miss Lister always wore, whatever the weather, over her shoulders and throat. By the standards of any fire department it wasn't really much of a blaze nor was the old lady badly injured, thanks to Elizabeth's prompt action in closing the door, shutting off the draught, and in smothering the flames with a thick tablecloth she snatched from the occasional table, regardless of the possible sentimental value this might have for the old lady.

It was all over very quickly. Michael had rushed downstairs in the wake of the two nurses, and Bill had pounded up from his basement, rushing back again for the huge First Aid kit he kept just inside his domain.

The burns were superficial, but Miss Lister was badly shocked, and although she pleaded not to be sent away Michael insisted that she should be taken into Jude's at least overnight until it had been established that there was nothing more to be done save to await the healing hand of time.

'I bet Mrs Lloyd'd have panicked, wouldn't she?' Joan said a trifle maliciously as the three of them stood together to wave as Miss Lister was driven away, moments later. Michael stared at her for a long moment without saying a word, then he shrugged.

'The fire might have upset her,' he said, at last, 'but panicking's something unknown to Ann. She's not the type. Might have been better for her if she hadn't been so well versed in self-control!' he said inexplicably.

Joan turned away. She had the strangest feeling that somehow, although without quite knowing how, she had been put in her place, and that in Michael Lloyd's opinion that place wasn't very high up in his scale of values!

'It sounds as though he'd have thought more of her if she'd been a little less self-contained,' she said as she regarded Elizabeth's lightly bandaged hands intently. 'I must say he's done a marvellous job on your hands, *and* on Miss Lister's shoulder, though fortunately she's only scorched, I think. He looked as though he'd have liked to fold you up in his arms, burns, bandages and all, Liz,' she teased, but Elizabeth wasn't amused.

'Don't be silly!' she said impatiently. 'He's had a hard enough day without having to meet up with this sort of thing when he gets home for a well deserved rest! Bill'll have to see the owner about those stoves and things. I'm sure there's some economical way of heating food— what little Miss Lister cooks for herself, for instance— without going to such dangerous lengths! She could have burned to death if there'd been no one else in the house!'

'Did you hear Michael when Mrs Forrest suggested it

was time Miss Lister went into one of the Homes?' Joan asked, still thinking of the look in Michael Lloyd's eyes as he had tenderly dealt with the burned tissue on Elizabeth's fingers where she had crushed out the flames.

'No,' Elizabeth hadn't been listening. She had been too conscious of the pounding of her heart, the pulsing of her blood as Michael's hands had held her own . . . that and his nearness had made her, she was surprised to feel, suddenly faint.

'It's because I'm extra tired,' she told herself firmly, then, with an effort, she forced herself to listen to Joan.

'I didn't hear it all,' Joan confessed, 'but it was something about there being other people, not all as wise or as stable as Miss Lister, who ought to be removed to a place where an eye can be kept on their movements. I think he was meaning that Mrs Forrest goes out too much and leaves the young twins to that girl of hers. She's making the child an old woman before she's a young one, and it isn't fair. I thought that sort of thing went out with the First World War.'

'I don't suppose there being two kinds of human beings will ever go out,' Elizabeth sighed. 'There are more than two kinds of human being, I know, but it always strikes me there are those who'll willingly be put upon and those who'll equally willingly put on them! That's human nature, and I don't suppose anything'll ever change that!'

Inevitably her thoughts returned to Michael Lloyd. Was he the kind to always willingly have people 'use' him, and was Mrs Lloyd the opposite kind of person, who would equally willingly accept all he offered and give in return scarcely even a gracious word of thanks?

'She looks as though she really doesn't care what happens to him in any way,' Elizabeth mused. 'Whatever went wrong it must have gone wrong with about the biggest bang possible. By the look of things I don't think they'll ever be able to get back to normal, whatever "normal" was for them!'

Long after the rest of Landawne House was asleep, Elizabeth lay awake. Her hands were not too painful, although the dressing Michael had used on them had made her skin slightly prickly and it took a great deal of concentration to prevent herself from tearing at the bandages and scratching.

'And that would be fatal, as well as being deliberately ungrateful to Michael for all the prompt care he took!' she reminded herself. 'I think I'll take another aspirin. I ought to be able to sleep a little then!'

She started as the sound of the car Dr Bickersley had hired for a time broke the silence. Tonight Mrs Lloyd did not linger, but within minutes was running upstairs, apparently, for once, making no effort to disguise the sound of her return. Elizabeth glanced at her watch. It was early for Mrs Lloyd to be returning, only a little after one o'clock. Had something gone wrong? Was there to be yet more trouble for Michael on top of his exhausting day at St Jude's and all that had happened since his return to the flat?

Elizabeth sat on the edge of her bed, unconsciously listening for any sounds which might emerge from flat five. She had not long to wait. The windows of both flats were open to the warm night air, and suddenly, reflected in the glass of her own window, Elizabeth saw the lights blazing from both bedrooms and from the living room of the Lloyds' flat.

Unaware of how tensely she was sitting, it was a severe shock to her nervous system when, abruptly, she heard Michael's voice, obviously raised in some argument. He did not sound angry, she realised. As usual, he sounded more resigned than hurt, and her heart ached for him and his apparent unhappiness.

'He must love her a great deal to put up with this sort of thing night after night, day after day,' she thought miserably. 'He *must* know the entire staff—and some of the patients—are discussing his affairs, and it can't be very rewarding for a man in a position such as his. If she doesn't care about herself, then she ought to think of him, whether she still loves him or not.'

She heard Ann's voice then, not loud enough for her to be able to distinguish the words, but loud enough for her to recognise that an argument was in progress, and an argument Ann seemed determined to win, cost what it may.

'It's not because he's weak,' Elizabeth told herself fiercely. 'Mum used to say there were people like that, people who gave so much of themselves to one person that they became victims of their own generosity. I bet he can't refuse her anything. And whatever it is she's set her mind on now, it sounds as though she's not going to give up until he's agreed, whether he wants to or not, poor soul! I'd like to tell him she might think more of him if he . . . stood up to her, told her what she must do and what she must not do, and saw to it she did as she was told . . .' but she knew that even had she been given the sudden power to affect the change she was thinking about, she would not have used it. Michael Lloyd, in any different guise save the one in which she felt she knew him so well, would not be the same man. He was, she had thought of more than once, the very epitome of Chaucer's 'perfect gentle knight', and a different Michael would not be the same in any way.

She hugged her knees, ignoring her bandaged hands. In her own bed in the far corner of the room, Joan stirred and muttered in her sleep before settling off again. Next door Ann's voice went on and on, then suddenly Michael spoke again.

He did not shout, and he did not say more than two or three sentences, then, to Elizabeth's horror, there was the unmistakable sound of a woman weeping. It wasn't like a normal bout of crying. There was something so deeply hurt, something which sounded remotely like a wounded animal trying desperately to hide itself from its fellow creatures, that Elizabeth felt as though her heart had turned completely over.

Michael spoke again, even now he was not angry. From the subdued murmur, for such it seemed after the raised voices of a few minutes ago, he appeared to be offering conciliatory terms.

'He's giving in to her, whatever it is,' Elizabeth thought, and it took all her determination not to make some sort of noise—any noise—and to let them know someone was awake and had heard.

'It's none of my business,' she reminded herself again, but she knew in her heart that it *was* her business, very much so. It was her affair just as much as it was theirs, and for one simple reason. She hadn't realised it before, but as though a curtain had been torn aside and what it had concealed had been revealed, she knew why she cared so much, and why she so much wanted Michael Lloyd to be happy.

She, Elizabeth Fletcher, the girl who had long ago

made up her mind that a career came before a love-life, was in love, really in love, for the first time in her life. And the man she loved was next door, arguing—or consoling—with the woman who stood between Elizabeth and what she knew now would be the realisation of all her girlhood dreams.

CHAPTER SIX

THE knowledge of why Michael's happiness mattered so greatly to her broke like a thunderclap on Elizabeth's outraged senses. She rose quietly and padded over to the kitchen corner, quietly making herself a restoring cup of tea. It wouldn't help her to sleep, but, she smiled wryly at her own reflections, as Sister Watson under whom she had done the first part of her training, had often said: ''Tis such a morale restorer, it's worth not being able to sleep after it! And when you're on night duty it's an essential! Ought to be part of issue, like in the Forces!'

Elizabeth knew nothing of the truth of that statement, but she did know the 'morale-restoring' qualities of the hot, strong sweetened liquid.

Cup in hand, she sat staring out into the lighting sky, watching the sun rise over the horizon, and wondering just what effect her self-discovery was likely to have on her life in the near future.

'He must love her,' she decided, even though every fibre of her being cried out against that knowledge. 'He wouldn't put up with a life like this, not all the time, unless he loved her very much. She's stupid—she must be—to throw away something as wonderful as this. And I'm stupid as well. Pretending to myself I've wanted to stay on here, to help him, just because he works at Jude's and happens to be my next-door neighbour! I ought to have known long ago. One doesn't concern oneself quite so much with just anybody!'

She sat still for a long time, her fingers curled round the cooling liquid in the cup. She stared unseeingly at the tangle of roof-tops and chimney pots spread out before her and emerging more and more clearly in the growing light.

If she stayed on at St Jude's there was a chance—a slim one, but a chance all the same—that one day she might be successful in the position of Assistant Matron, since rumour had it Assistant Matron Starke was going to be married in the autumn.

'There's nothing to prevent my applying,' she reflected, 'and I should imagine I'd stand as good a chance as anyone else who might apply here.'

She thought back over her own record. On reflection it was quite good. She had her SRN, her RMN and midwifery. She'd been Nurse of the Year the year she qualified, and so far she'd done nothing to bring down the wrath and disapproval of the authorities on her head.

But did she want to stay here . . . now? Could she carry on, viewing the situation impartially, knowing Michael Lloyd wasn't a happy man, and didn't seem likely ever to be happy while he and Ann were together?

'I don't think I could stand it,' she reasoned. 'Not watching things go from bad to worse, and it's evident that that's what they are doing, if they've taken to quarrelling when she comes home!'

There wasn't a sound from number five now, and the lights had been switched out long ago. Still Elizabeth sat on, her tea forgotten as she stared into the growing daylight and tried to remember what life had been like before Michael and Ann Lloyd came to St Jude's.

'I was happy then, and I didn't realise it,' she remembered. Sometimes, when Joan had been bewailing Tim's lack of interest, and she, Elizabeth, had been more than a little bored by the attentions of one or another of the young men who'd clamoured to take her out, she had scoffed at the whole idea of love.

'There can't be just one particular person for everyone,' she remembered her own arguments quite well. 'It stands to reason there are types, and that one particular type will always seek out its couplement. But there's more than one person of every type. There must be, and that's why people who lose their life-partners so often marry again, someone almost exactly like their previous partner . . . it's just that they are attracted to that particular kind.'

Joan had argued fiercely there was one person for everyone, and that when one found one's own partner then it was one's bounden duty to move heaven and earth to get together. That was what Joan had done, because she was so certain she and Tim O'Toole were made for one another. She had even, Elizabeth smiled to herself, stuck most rigidly to a diet and exercises in order to achieve and preserve the face and form Tim admired.

Where she was concerned, Elizabeth reflected unhappily, there was a far more substantial barrier than mere flesh and form between herself and happiness!

She sighed and set down the now-cold tea. For a moment she toyed with the idea of making a fresh one, but decided against it. She would take an aspirin—not a wise thing to do at this hour, since it might well produce the sleep which had so far evaded her—and then she would sleep too soundly and too long. Far better, she decided, to go to bed and deliberately practise the relaxation exercises which she had taught herself to so many patients.

It was strange, she thought, once more in bed, how when one taught someone something which was deliberately constructed to help them one grew a little frustrated, even if one didn't show it, when the patient failed to respond. Now, deliberately trying to imagine her limbs heavy and weighted, beginning at her toes and deliberately following the muscles all the way up her limbs to her middle, she could well sympathise.

It took a sheer effort of will to accomplish what it had always seemed so easy to teach, but at long last a feeling of drowsiness crept over her, her senses dulled, even to the twitter of the house sparrows which were chattering noisily in the guttering outside the window, and she slept. She wakened to the shrilling of the alarm clock. This time there was no hesitation. She was out of bed immediately, as usual, and padding off to the kitchen to put on the kettle. It was as though the brief, intense sleep had restored more than a calm of mind. It had helped her arrive at some sort of decision, but even as she thought of this doubts began to steal into her mind.

Was the decision the right one? What effect would it have on Joan and her future? What would Michael Lloyd think when she went away, not for a time, but for ever?

'He won't think anything,' she told herself firmly, pouring the boiling water from the kettle. 'He'll perhaps wonder what sort of neighbours he'll have next, but no more than that. Joan'll either find someone else to share the lease or decide to move back into the Home until she and Tim are married. I wonder . . .'

'I shall be glad when it's Change-Over again,' she remarked as she seated herself opposite to Joan and began to eat her cereal. 'I've had a white night. It's years since I had one, and I think it's a sign it's time I was due for a spell on night duty again, don't you?'

'I hate nights,' Joan said decisively. 'Things never seem in the same sort of perspective after a week or so. I'd rather be normal and sleep when the rest of the world is sleeping, doing my odds and ends in that part of the twenty-four hours which seems deliberately planned to do all that's necessary . . . not that I'm saying night duty isn't necessary. It is. It's just that . . . well, daft as it might sound, I was once washing out some stockings after coming off a night shift, and it struck me how ridiculous it was, when everyone with a normal sort of job would be just getting up and preparing to go to work for the day, and there was I, preparing to go to bed!'

'And I love nights . . . in their turn,' Elizabeth was speaking the truth, as Joan was well aware. 'I like the quiet of the wards. Sometimes in the day it's more like a free-for-all than a hospital ward, so many people coming and going, so much rush and bustle. In the night one has a chance to chat with those patients who, for one reason or another, can't sleep. Sometimes it's a help . . . to both patient and to the nurse.'

'How?' Joan demanded. 'To the nurse, I mean.'

'Sometimes,' Elizabeth said reflectively, 'one finds a patient can't sleep not because of pain or discomfort, but because of some private worry at home, for example. Lot's of them don't realise the Almoner's there to help, or half the things she can do if she gets to know about them. A quiet chat with the nurse, in the whispered intimacy of the night hours, often helps a patient to unburden herself, to get the advice she or he would never otherwise have sought, and, in the long run, renders complete recovery a far quicker affair than it normally would be.'

'I like people,' Joan opined, 'but I haven't all your sympathy, love. I'll listen, if there's anything practical I can do to help, like arranging a water bed, having extra warmth . . . anything like that, but when it comes to sympathy with the reason why X's mum won't be there on visiting day, well, I'm afraid I feel more than just inclined to tell them I'm there to *nurse* them, not to sort out their private worries as well.'

'That's part of nursing, I think,' Elizabeth wasn't lecturing, just speaking her thoughts aloud. 'I like to *know* about people, know why they are worrying, and if there is anything at all I can do to help them sort out whatever it is. I'm a firm believer in psychosomatic medicine, as you know. I think a number of illnesses are caused more by people's emotions and thoughts than by the actual viruses or bugs or what-have-you.'

'Comes of taking your RMN,' Joan asserted cheerfully. 'Why all this introspection at this hour of the morning, anyhow?'

'Just wondering what will happen when Assistant Matron leaves,' Elizabeth said lightly. 'There was a time . . .'

'When you'd have thought of applying for the position, is that it?' Joan demanded as she paused. 'And now?' as Elizabeth nodded.

'Now . . . I just don't know,' she admitted with disarming simplicity. 'In fact I don't know whether or not I really want to stay on at Jude's, especially as you and Tim'll soon be getting married.'

'Your indecision hasn't anything to do with our friend in the flat across the way, by any remote chance, has it?'

Joan queried, and as the slow colour rose in Elizabeth's cheeks she nodded.

'I thought as much,' she said quietly. 'I've seen this coming, and there hasn't been a blinking thing I could do about it. It's no good, Liz, not with someone of your principles! With someone like me it wouldn't matter so much. If I wanted him,' her tone strengthened and she looked, Elizabeth decided with inward amusement, so thoroughly determined that she seemed an entirely different person, 'I'd fight like mad, especially when it's as plain as a pike-staff he can't possibly be happy as he's situated. What man could be happy, never a moment of proper home-life and not really one of the boys, as Tim has it, living in Jude's entirely.'

Elizabeth thought of the raised voices during the night, and of the sound of Mrs Lloyd's weeping and of his conciliatory tones. What man, indeed, could be happy in such a circumstance? Yet she said nothing at all of this to Joan now. Joan, she felt, dear soul though she was, would not understand!

'So you're thinking of running away, then?' Joan asked as they closed the door of the flat and hurried for the bus stop. Time had flown as they had chatted, and now there was not time for the usual walk to Jude's.

'I think it might be as well,' Elizabeth answered slowly. 'I can give in my notice, though it won't be accepted for this month. It'll have to be August now, and I'll be free on September the first. Take a vacation then—the one I should be taking in late August and early September, and then hope I'm in at which ever hospital seems the most suitable.'

'That being?' Joan pressed as the bus stopped at their stop.

'The one most distant from Malenchester,' Elizabeth said briefly. 'I think I'll try either London or really way up North. Or I might even try for my Queen's and then go on District. That ought to be a change, *and* interesting.'

'The same could be said of the missionary field, but I wouldn't fancy my chances,' Joan said as they walked into the day staff cloakroom and changed for the day. 'Don't do anything rash, Liz. Not today, anyhow. I've just remembered a little whisper Mary told me the middle of last week. There may be nothing in it, and on the other hand it may make all the difference to your plans. Wait until we've had a chat after duty this evening. See you!'

They parted company and Elizabeth went first to see to those of her patients so far not affected by the influenza virus. She didn't want to be taken from being in touch with them. To Elizabeth a patient was a 'person' from the moment she or he came under her care, and she hated it when anything like the present epidemic interfered with her normal routine.

Mrs Andrews, a middle-aged woman suffering from chronic myocarditis, was an especial friend of hers. The woman had been into Jude's several times, and she had often said it was 'like coming back to a friend to find you still here, Sister.'

Mrs Andrews had experienced a white night too, as she was at great pains to explain to Elizabeth, who felt she could well and truly sympathise this time.

She settled the woman more comfortably, made a note to ask the houseman to take a further respiratory test and to write up something to alleviate the dyspnoea which had occurred, then she went on to the next bed.

She was a little astonished to find Mrs Elliot back and to learn that her husband had found her in a coma.

'Thought she was cured,' Staff Arnold remarked crisply. 'And of course she's not kept to her diet, wouldn't call in Dr Meredith, so she's back with us again. It's my belief she wanted to get back under Dr Lloyd's eye. She seems to have some sort of a fixation about him, but she's not the only one . . . amongst the patients, I mean. It's that sympathetic air that's responsible.'

Elizabeth could well understand the feeling. The chart told her the woman had already had a hundred and fifty units of soluble insulin and that she was written up for a further fifty.

'Her last Fehling's test was three and a half per cent glycosuria,' Staff said. 'Dr Lloyd said she should be all right after this bottle of saline, but to stick another one up if this one gives out before he's round again.'

Elizabeth completed the round, then went through the ritual of barrier nursing before entering the epidemic ward. Crisis point appeared to have been passed here, but there were two new admissions, both seriously ill.

There were no further cases of the epidemic influenza admitted that day, and it was with some relief she heard Michael, when he made his final round, say that in his opinion as well as in that of the MOH for Malenchester, the crisis was over.

'I should like to congratulate you and your nurses on the magnificent effort you have made to cope with a crisis of this nature especially at this time of the year, when one isn't quite so prepared for it as in the early spring or midwinter, Sister,' he said gravely as Elizabeth walked with him from the ward. 'Matron was pleased, when we talked this morning, by the way her staff had reacted. I could have told her most of the credit ought to go to her Sisters for the wonderful lead they had given the nurses, but I think she knew.'

It was ridiculous to feel so warmed by such faint praise, but Elizabeth *did*. She was smiling faintly as she went back to her desk, and she didn't even feel foolish when she caught Nurse Somers looking at her in a speculative manner.

Why should she leave here? she asked herself. What if Michael Lloyd and Mrs Lloyd couldn't manage their own affairs better than they were doing? Was it going to be of any help to any of the three of them if she moved out and left him to endure whatever it was he had to endure without even her friendship?

'It isn't that, and you know it!' she reproved herself sternly. 'What's worrying you is can you bear to move so far away from him, so out of touch, that you won't know just what is happening and whether or not things will work out for him?' Yet honesty compelled her to admit, though only to her innermost mind, that that wasn't the whole of it either.

Could she bear to stay on at Jude's, seeing him every day, working with him, listening to his voice, watching for his entrance into her ward and accompanying him from bed to bed, and all the time wondering what it would be like to have his arms about her, to have that thin, clever face bending over her own?

Could she bear to lie awake at night, listening for the sound of Mrs Lloyd's return from one or the other of her excursions out with the gay Dr Bickersley, and wanting to comfort Michael, knowing she hadn't the right?

She didn't know which would be the worst to bear,

being out of touch and miles away, or being close and unable to do anything to help make him happy . . . and herself too, for that matter. It was a problem which had no part of her routine life at St Jude's, however, and with a brisk admonition to herself to put first things first she made an unexpected swoop on the sluice room, the ward kitchens and on any and everything else she could think of, working off some of her frustration in this mundane way.

By the time she returned to the flat she was so tired that, emotions or not, she knew she would sleep that night, and without the help of even one aspirin.

Joan, arriving home rather later, whirled into the flat like a whirlwind, demanding almost instantly to know whether or not Elizabeth had done or said anything which might lead people to believe she was to leave Jude's.

'Haven't had time to give much thought to it today,' Elizabeth confessed. 'I did bring the *Nursing Mirror* home. I thought I'd look down the lists and see if there was anything really attractive going, anywhere I'd fancy going.'

'Then don't look until later, if you still want to look at all,' Joan advised. 'I thought I'd heard aright, but I wasn't sure. Mary confirmed the rumour this morning, and now I've had it from Tim as well, and he knows, so it isn't a rumour after all, it's just plain fact.'

'What is?' Elizabeth asked.

'That Dr Bickersley's leaving St Jude's at the end of this month,' Joan said with triumph. 'Don't ask me why, or how he's managed to be here for such a short stay, it's far too complicated to understand. It's something to do with some work he's been doing for the World Health

Organisation, and I understand he's going back there, probably out somewhere in the East, or so Tim says. He's a clever chap, I'll give him that, but . . .'

'Exactly,' Elizabeth said dryly. 'But . . .' and in both their minds was the thought that if Dr Bickersely went away, perhaps there would be, at last, an opportunity for some sort of a happy life for Doctor and Mrs Lloyd.

Joan evidently thought so, and had no hesitation in expressing her opinion.

'It stands to reason that with her boy-friend out of the way she'll have *some* time and energy to spare for Dr Lloyd, by way of a change,' she said, happily clattering pots and pans in her earnest endeavours to 'learn to knock up a meal the way you do' before she married Tim in the autumn.

'And what if she's even more withdrawn and aloof when he's gone?' Elizabeth wondered, but not aloud. She was remembering that it was not until Dr Roland Bickersley had come to Jude's that Mrs Lloyd had seemed to come alive. Prior to his arrival she had been like an animated statue, walking about the corridors of Landawne House, or Jude's, as though she were simply a clockwork machine, wound up and set to do a certain amount of duty before the works ran down and required rewinding.

With Dr Bickersley gone, Elizabeth wondered, might there be some chance for happiness for Michael after all? And if there was, could she bear to stay on at Jude's and watch it . . . see him relaxed and glowing in the comfort of his own home and with his own woman? Alternatively, could she bear to be miles away and not even in touch, and never knowing, apart from the scrappy letters she knew Joan would send wherever she went until she became too involved in her own happiness to bother any more, how things were with him?

This was back to square one with a vengeance. Her application for the post of Assistant Matron would have to be in within the next week, if she were to make it. Alternatively her notice must be handed in by the same date, if she decided to leave Jude's after all.

She went to bed early, but not to sleep. And when, in the early hours of the morning, she heard Ann Lloyd returning home, she was no nearer making a decision than she had been when she fell asleep.

CHAPTER SEVEN

ELIZABETH had made no decision when, two days later, she encountered Michael Lloyd in the lift as she returned home at the end of the day. Change-Over would be due at the weekend, and now, more than ever, she was looking forward—although with mixed feelings—to being back on night shift.

The mingled feelings were all mixed up with her indecision about Michael Lloyd. If she were on night duty, then she would not lie awake, listening for the return of Mrs Lloyd, noting, almost automatically now, what hour she arrived home and how long she and Dr Bickersley sat talking in the car outside Landawne House.

'Whatever they talk about it must be important,' Elizabeth reasoned to herself, 'at least so far as they are concerned. But is it necessary? And how on earth does she manage to do her job properly?' although that question was partly answered when she happened to sit beside Staff OP on the way home one evening.

'Your new neighbour doesn't seem to be with it very much these days,' the other said succinctly. 'She's got her mind on something—or someone—else, I should imagine. We're all having to carry her these days. Is there anything wrong?'

Elizabeth, from some sense of loyalty to Michael, stoutly asserted that all was well, so far as she was aware, with her neighbours, but her heart ached as she thought of the reserved, shy Dr Lloyd being the subject of the usual grapevine gossip, and through no fault of his own.

Standing beside him in the wonky old lift, smiling in return of his greeting, she wondered whether or not she could ask him in for a coffee. He stepped aside for her to leave the lift first, and then startled her by asking outright if he might come in for a minute.

'Of course.' Elizabeth was delighted, her own small problem solved for her. 'I was wondering if you'd like a coffee.'

'That would be most kind,' he said formally, 'but I really wanted to talk to you.'

Comfortably settled in the chair he always seemed to favour, and with a cup of the steaming, fragrant coffee beside him, Michael seemed in no hurry to begin. Elizabeth resisted the temptation to start the preparations of the evening meal and sat quietly beside him, waiting for whatever it was he wanted to talk about. At last, when he spoke, his first remark did not appear to make very much sense.

'What do you think of the theory that if a man—say a pilot in a war—had a crash and is sent up straight away in a plane, always assuming, of course, he hadn't been injured, in order to "get his nerve back", is the phrase, I believe . . . do you think it's a good idea, generally applied to ordinary living, I mean?' he asked.

'You mean . . . another example,' Elizabeth smiled, 'if someone was learning to ride a horse and fell off, shocking but not injuring themselves, ought they immediately to remount? Is that it?'

'Something like that,' he admitted, 'although the problem I'm thinking of has nothing to do with either horses or aeroplanes. It's more an emotional one.'

'I think it's a very sound one—in theory, of course,' she said solemnly. 'I've never experienced anything even remotely like that myself, but I think one's logic says that unless one retackles a problem, be it a horse, aeroplane or examination, after one failure or mishap, one is likely to be left with a fear of that particular thing and, if it should ever reoccur without warning, one might well go to pieces.'

'In brief, then, you'd advise anyone faced with such a problem to have a go, Elizabeth?' he queried, and there was so much anxious enquiry behind the few simple words she knew she would have agreed with him, merely to reassure him, whatever her own feelings had been.

'I rather think I would,' she said quietly. 'I hope that's enough to help?'

'It is.' He was very grave. 'It's helped me make up my mind about what to say on . . . a certain point which has been bothering me for weeks. I think—I hope—you're right. You usually are, I've discovered! Thanks.'

Elizabeth wasn't sure what he was thanking her for, but it was a relief to see his expression had lightened and that some of the look of anxiety had gone from his eyes. It was also, in some strange way, a relief to herself, for she knew now that no matter what Mrs Lloyd and Dr Bickersley might do, she would not leave St Jude's, not yet, anyway. She would stay and see what happened to Ann and Michael once Dr Bickersley had returned to wherever he had come from.

This was a resolve it proved far easier to make than to act upon. All that week she worked automatically, and as, one by one, the gastro-enteritis cases were cleared from the wards and the hospital gradually returned fully to normal routine, she began to feel the entire episode had assumed a dreamlike quality and that it had not been real at all.

Dr Bickersley and Ann Lloyd appeared to be as immersed in one another as they had been from the first day of his arrival at St Jude's. Now, when she left Out-Patients, after a quick cup of tea or coffee and a roll at the canteen, he would be waiting for her, and they would drive off, Ann not even returning to Landawne House until well after midnight.

Mary Walker, whom Elizabeth encountered one day along the corridor, was avid for any details she might be able to pick up, but Elizabeth, although she liked the elderly ward maid normally, was annoyed to think Michael and his affairs were the subject of gossip, whether of a malicious nature or not and cut short the other's guarded enquiry as to how 'Dr Lloyd's managing, living half in and half out of Jude's, as you might say.'

Almost curtly Elizabeth said it was no concern of hers, and that Dr Lloyd appeared satisfied with his life the way it was. Then she reminded Mary about some neglected dusting—knowing full well that since the improved cleaning equipment had been installed a year or so ago, the dusting and polishing of the ward was more than up to standard.

Mary, however, was a psychologist in her own amateur way. She didn't resent the implied rebuke, but when the Sister had gone on her way she stood for a long minute looking after her retreating form and clicking her tongue against her teeth, an annoying habit she had when she was thinking.

'Nurse Barstow was right, after all,' she told herself, glad to think of the cheerful exchange of gossip she would have with Joan the next time they met in the course of their work. 'Sister *does* think more of Dr Lloyd than she'll admit, even to herself. It's a pity Mrs Lloyd's such a nice young woman as well! It's made it a sight easier to make things difficult for her if she was someone a body could take a dislike to, but that's life, I suppose!' and ruminating on the queer way in which some people appeared to work out their fate, as she thought of it, Mary picked up her mop and went on her way.

It was not quite as simple as that for Elizabeth. Half her mind was angry because Ann Lloyd left opportunity for gossip about the doctor and didn't appear to mind, and the other half was telling herself firmly that 'maybe I can help him . . . later,' although when 'later' was likely to occur she couldn't imagine. Vaguely she knew it must have some connection with the talk she and Michael had had about whether or not one should advise someone to repeat what had been a painful experience or not. More than that she was not certain about, but there was some connection, she was sure.

Next week, she realised, she would be on night duty. This change-over did not come about, for the Sisters, as regularly as when she had been a newly qualified nurse, or even a staff nurse. Then the change-over had only come at three-monthly intervals at Jude's. After that there had been the experiment of permanent night and day staffing of Sisters and staff nurses, but after one hectic night when a multiple crash on the nearby motor-way had resulted in two of the then permanent night staff being off sick for a period, Matron had worked out another routine, and a change-over was made every six months.

Strangely enough she wasn't sure now that she was

going to welcome the change as much as she had anticipated. She would not know, not for another six months,
how often Ann Lloyd stayed out late or who looked after
Michael when he arrived home, and who could say what
might happen before the six months ended?

One thing which she knew *would* happen, since
arrangements had already been put in hand to that
effect, was that Joan would no longer be sharing the flat
with her. Tim's small share in the group practice he had
hoped for had materialised, and he and Joan were
happily planning their marriage for the middle of
September.

Whether she would want to stay on in Landawne
House without Joan as a companion, Elizabeth did not
know. To leave, even to go into the Nurses' Home and
have her own room on the Sisters' floor would be the
easy answer, but she would have put a further gap
between herself and Michael, and, unhappy though she
was in this present arrangement, she knew she didn't
want to erect any further barrier between them.

She was thinking about this as she entered Landawne
House one evening, coming off duty. A huge taxi had
drawn up at the doors, and the burly driver was already
lifting a large suitcase into his cab. Across the road was
the hired car in which Dr Bickersley whisked Mrs Lloyd
to and fro almost daily, and Liz felt as though a cold
hand had clutched at her heart as she walked into the
house.

Bill, walking downstairs, greeted her as she entered,
with the not unusual news that, 'The lift's gone off again,
Nurse. I keep on at 'em, but they don't seem to bother. I
reckon Mrs Lloyd's right when she says the only way to
impress the owners is to have a rent strike by all the

tenants! That'll make 'em have it seen to, I'll bet!'

Elizabeth sympathised and said she didn't hold with strikes, but that it must be infuriating to Bill when his work entailed so many journeys up and down the stairs.

'I don't mind,' he said, once more as grave as ever. 'It's good exercise, normal-like. It's when folks are movin' out or in it's a bit tiresome. Still, I reckon that's the lot. I'll be back soon, if the doctor comes in and wants anything. It's my day for collecting my pension, you know.'

Relieved, Elizabeth bade him a cheerful 'cheerio', knowing he would have to walk smartly to reach the post-office before it closed and that he wouldn't, this time, want to stand and chat.

Half-way upstairs she encountered Ann Lloyd descending, her coat and hat over one arm, her small case held in her other hand. Only then did she realise what Bill had meant by 'that's the lot'. There had been a small collection of cases, packages and parcels in the hall, a collection the driver of the cab was already stacking neatly inside.

Ann Lloyd looked down at Elizabeth and Elizabeth looked back. For a moment neither spoke, then unexpectedly Ann held out her hand.

'I'll say goodbye, if I may,' she said coolly, in the low, musical voice Elizabeth had heard so seldom since Ann had come to live as her neighbour.

'I don't suppose we shall meet again,' she went on, 'but I'd like to thank you for being so kind to Michael. It hasn't been easy for him, and I know his talks with you have meant a great deal to him all these weeks.'

Elizabeth was astounded. Automatically—and merely because, as she thought of it afterwards—she had been brought up to do the right thing, she took Ann's hand and shook it.

'Goodbye,' she said, equally automatically. 'I . . . I hope you'll be happy.'

'I'm sure I shall,' Ann said quickly as though trying to reassure herself. 'I know now this is what I should have done all those months ago, but I was too much of a coward.'

Elizabeth stood where she was as Ann went on down the stairs. She saw her enter the taxi and the driver shut the door, then the cab drove away, and almost immediately the hired car from across the road followed. Elizabeth went slowly to her own flat and took off her outdoor things. What on earth had happened? Where was Ann going, and why? And in what way did she imagine Elizabeth's brief talks with Michael had been any help to him?

'I suppose she thinks he's been telling me all about her and Roland Bickersley,' she decided as she set to work to prepare the evening meal. 'She's wrong! He's never mentioned them. I wonder if he knows they've gone off together? Surely he'd have been here, or something, if he'd known . . . it's all very queer.'

Her own meal and Joan's was almost ready to serve when someone tapped on her door. It was almost a shock when she opened it to see Michael Lloyd standing there, and a complete surprise when he looked so unexpectedly happy.

'I wonder if you could let me have a little milk, please?' he began. 'Ann appears to have forgotten to go down for any, and Bill's out. I'll return it later.'

'That's all right.' Elizabeth felt awkward, and didn't know how to face him, looking so happy and contented, apparently believing Ann was either still at Jude's or simply that she had, as he said, simply forgotten he would be home.

'You can eat with us if you like,' she offered. 'There's plenty, and it will save you the trouble of having to get anything else ready . . .' She had been about to add 'for yourself', but somehow the words would not come. She couldn't be the one to wipe that look of happiness from his face, a look which had not been there very often throughout all the time she had known him.

'If you're certain it won't make a great deal of extra work for you,' he accepted. 'I'd love to come . . . there's no one home but myself, you see.'

'I know,' Elizabeth said briefly. How could she tell him Ann had just taken all her things—or had he not had time enough to look round and see that for himself—and gone off with Roland Bickersley, the man everyone was saying would be leaving at the end of the month? Whatever happened, Elizabeth resolved, he should have at least one peaceful hour. She wouldn't mention Ann or the fact that she had gone. Let him relax and have a meal in peace. Time enough for him to worry about Ann and her affairs when he'd eaten and settled down a little after his busy, work-filled day.

She chatted lightly as she completed the preparations for the meal, adding a table setting for a third person, adding more fruit to the bowl on the table, cutting more bread and butter.

Michael sat, relaxed and at ease, answering as she spoke, but saying nothing which would give her a convenient opening which would enable her to break the news gently, if such news could be broken gently, she reflected.

'There were a number of strange stories floating round at St Jude's this morning,' he said, pulling out a battered-looking pipe and beginning to stuff it with tobacco. 'Do you mind?' he waved the thing vaguely in her direction.

'Not in the least,' Elizabeth assured him truthfully. 'I like to see a man with a pipe. Dad always used one, and somehow I always associate pipe-smokers with the symbols of quiet security. Utter nonsense, of course, except that in all honesty I must confess most pipe-smokers seem the more placid-natured members of your sex.'

'We are,' Michael affirmed, smiling. 'That's why so many people take advantage of us, you know. They realise it won't matter in the long run, we'll . . . give in.'

He sounded as he had been accustomed to sound, resigned and a trifle unsure of himself. It was time, Elizabeth decided, to at least attempt to change the subject and to restore his previous seeming contentment.

'What sort of strange stories were you referring to a moments ago?' she asked, whipping up the salad dressing. Whatever they were, she told herself, they couldn't have anything to do with Ann, since there had been no one, save Dr Bickersley, present when the other girl had departed. 'And he seems to come and go as he pleases,' Elizabeth reflected, 'so no one'll have missed him very much!'

'Well,' Michael seemed to be making a great business of the lighting of his pipe, and when it appeared to be well and truly alight he spoke again, although, she noticed, without looking at her.

'We all know Roland Bickersley's gone,' he said quietly. 'We all know Miss Sparke is to be married in the autumn. One of the stories I heard this morning—and it came from quite a reliable source and not one usually associated with the grapevine—was that if a certain fairly new Sister,' at this point she saw him raise his eyebrows in a strangely quizzical manner, 'were to apply, there is strong reason to suppose she would be accepted.'

Elizabeth said nothing. She was trying to think who on earth, except Joan, had known of her intention to apply for the position of Assistant Matron, should it become vacant during her stay at Jude's.

There were too many people who knew, she decided. Tim had known, and had said he thought she was an extremely likely candidate, and if he were making a book, he'd put his money on her. This had been his way of saying he approved and hoped she'd be accepted, should such a situation arise. In the days when he had made this speech, however, Miss Sparke had not even been engaged, and the subject had arisen when Elizabeth, as usual, had been holding forth on the advantages of selecting one career at the outset and making the best possible use of all angles relating to that career.

'I want to go on nursing as long as ever I can,' she remembered clearly making that statement when, to christen the then newly opened self-service canteen, a number of them had been grouped around two of the small tables pushed together, drinking coffee and eating the now famous rock doughnuts which had quickly become a feature, though not a popular one, of the service.

'There's no necessity to stop nursing, even if you marry,' Tim had said slowly, and, looking back, Elizabeth thought how blind both she and Joan had been, since the way in which he had looked at Joan when he made that particular statement should have told them both he was already attracted to the girl, and it must have been nothing more than her off-hand manner which had caused him to hesitate until, when she had embarked on her own course of self-improvement, he had been a great deal more forthcoming.

'I would,' Elizabeth remembered saying now. 'Nurses—real nurses—want to go on and on,' she had opined. 'I'm not meaning it's true of every girl who enters the profession. I'm speaking of the few, to whom it's more than a job, it's a way of life. That's what it is for me, and one I'd never really want to leave completely. I'd like,' she recalled her exact words, 'to go on and on. To become a Senior Sister here, then start to apply for an Assistant Matronship somewhere. No other hospital would be as good as Jude's, of course, not at first. The chances of Lorna Sparke ever leaving, unless it was to take a Matronship somewhere else, are as remote as my own chances of going round the world on a marvellous first-class cruise—another of my long-felt ambitions I don't suppose I shall ever see realised.'

'One never knows,' Tim had said enigmatically, and, much later, she remembered, it had been Tim who had first mentioned Lorna Sparke's hitherto unsuspected lover, overseas, with the Air Force.

'It must have been Tim,' she decided at this point, and was about to embark on her favourite topic of the kind of nurse she had always aimed at being and which she hoped she had succeeded in becoming, when Michael spoke again.

'If all that's true,' he said slowly, 'I don't suppose you'd ever be interested in part-time nursing, and living somewhere else . . . say on the coast somewhere, in a little market town?'

'I . . . I haven't had reason to think about that!' Elizabeth said, her colour rising as she wondered what, if anything, lay behind those few words.

Michael didn't comment on the single remark. Instead, looking round as though he expected to discover some clue, he added:

'I don't suppose you saw anything of Ann and Roland this morning, did you? They'd be gone before you came home, I expect. It doesn't matter really, because I shall see them tomorrow.'

For a moment Elizabeth could only stare, wide-eyed, in complete disbelief that he had actually *known* that Ann and Roland were about to go away together. She swallowed hard. There was an unexpected emotional lump in her throat as she recalled how distressed she had been such a short time ago, and entirely on his behalf.

'You mean that you *knew*?' she said incredulously. 'You actually knew they were . . . going away together, today, and you can sit there calmly and do nothing whatsoever about it?'

'Of course I knew!' Michael said placidly. 'As to doing anything about it, I thoroughly believe it's the best possible thing which could have happened, for both of them. I'm only sorry Roland didn't appear on the horizon at least six months sooner. We'd all have been spared a great deal of . . . shall we say, mental discomfort if he had!'

Elizabeth was frankly puzzled. He had looked happy when he arrived at the flat, his main concern being the fact that there wasn't any milk and that Bill was out so that he would have to wait to collect any Ann had remembered to order. He had continued to look happy, she remembered, and now he told her, quite calmly, that he had known all the time he would be returning to an empty flat yet once again, and that this time there didn't appear to be any sign of Ann's intended return.

'It's all for the best, Elizabeth,' he said gently. 'I know that to some people it may seem a rather drastic form of treatment, but my grandmother had a saying which was far more truthful than I would have believed possible in the days when I used to stand at her knee and imbibe her words of wisdom.'

Elizabeth stood in silence. She felt so completely at a loss it would have been impossible to find any words which would suit the occasion.

'Grandmother,' Michael continued placidly, puffing clouds of smoke into the air, 'used to say sometimes one had to kill to cure. I don't think it's as bad as that,' he smiled again, the slow, attractive smile, 'and I foresee them both coming back . . .'

Whatever he had been about to say was cut short in mid-sentence. From downstairs came the shrill, frightened screams of a child, the raised voices of two women, one Elizabeth recognised as being the quavering voice of Miss Lister.

'That's the Forrest woman,' Michael rose, knocking out his pipe. 'I expect she's left her brats with Miss Lister again and one of them had done something and she's blaming the old lady. Why she can't stay home and look after them herself, I don't know. It isn't that she has to go out to help make a living for them all. She goes out on pleasure bent, as Ann would have said, and then grumbles and complains when anyone who's been silly enough to accept the responsibilities which should have been hers finds it too difficult to cope.'

'They're a regular handful to *have* to cope with, by all accounts, too.' Elizabeth was tearing off the frilled apron she had donned to do her chores. She needed no urging whatsoever to follow Michael, who was already rushing downstairs, the lift again wearing its 'out-of-order' light.

They found the commotion was going on, as they had suspected, in Miss Lister's overcrowded room. The next to the youngest Forrest child was clutched tightly in his mother's arms, which appeared to have the entire opposite of a soothing effect, and was screaming and crying loudly enough to deafen anyone. Little Miss Lister was hovering anxiously about the pair, although it was impossible to see what she was trying to accomplish. As the doctor and nurse appeared in the doorway, the child's screams subsided to a painful crying and its small frame shook with half-choked sobs.

'I didn't know it was there until we came home and he began poking and making awful faces,' Miss Lister was saying over and over again.

'Anybody with any sense would have known better than to let a child his years roll about on grass when it's as high as all that!' Mrs Forrest protested. 'If he's lost his hearing, it's *your* fault, and no one else's. I should think I can have the law on you for this! I'll go round to the Citizens' Advice Bureau in the morning and find out what they have to say about it!'

'Take the child over to the window, please,' Michael spoke to the mother. His tone was quiet, but there was that air of authority about him which made her immediately do as he requested. As though requiring time to adjust himself to the change of scene and to the movement, the little boy ceased crying, and only the occasional loud gulping noise of choked back sobs indicated that all was not yet well with him.

'Tell me what happened,' Michael ordered next adding, as both women began to speak, 'and one at a time, if you don't mind. Miss Lister?'

'Mrs Forrest asked me if I'd have the two elder children for the afternoon,' she began, her elderly voice stronger now she was not so frightened herself. 'We went to the new small park, just down the road. We stayed by that little ornamental lake they have, the one with the fountain splashing into it, and usually a crowd of ducks and small waterfowl. I think they have their nests either on that little island almost in the middle, or in the reeds growing round it.'

'Yes,' Michael said, not abruptly, but again his tone was an indication that it was time to proceed.

'We left Roger, that's this little chap,' she smiled at the still sobbing toddler, 'lying on the grass. He was making a daisy-chain and wasn't interested in feeding the ducks as Deborah was. I could see him all the time,' she continued, her voice more firm as she stressed her non-neglect. 'We weren't away many minutes, just long enough for Debby to throw some crusts in for the ducks and to watch them come for them, then we went back to Roger. He was all right then,' she insisted. 'He was all right until we started on the way home.'

'And then?' Michael wasn't impatient, but seconds which may well prove to be precious ones were ticking away, and he was as yet no nearer learning exactly what had happened and with what he must be prepared to cope.

'We'd nearly reached the end of the road,' Miss Lister continued, 'when Roger began to cry and to hold his ear. I stopped the push-chair, of course, and told Debby to hold on to it . . . it gives her a sense of responsibility if I tell her she must be quite certain the push-chair doesn't run away,' she added pridefully.

No one said anything, and after a moment she continued, now becoming a little confused.

'Roger was still holding his ear and crying,' she said quietly. 'When I looked there was a small insect— probably a small beetle, I don't know, it was something I didn't recognise—just inside the ear.'

'And then?'

'I always carry two clean handkerchiefs,' Miss Lister stated. 'I tried to get the thing out . . .'

'And it retreated further into the ear. Is that it?' Michael asked, and the relief on Miss Lister's face was sufficient to prove his guess had been the right one.

'I'll take him up to my flat, if you don't mind.' Michael had taken charge. He turned to Elizabeth. 'I have my GP bag there, and I think we can cope with this pretty well without a great deal of trouble. You'll help, won't you?' He appeared to take her acceptance for granted and, lifting the child gently from its mother's arms, he began to lead the way. At the door he paused to say over his shoulder: 'If you two ladies will please stay down here we hope not to be very long. I think,' he gave a meaningful glance in Mrs Forrest's direction, 'this is a case where you ought to make a good cup of tea for Miss Lister and another for yourself. We'll be back, with Roger OK, before you have had time to drink it.'

Elizabeth followed him into flat five. It was the first time she had been inside this flat since Molly and Ian

Frazer left. The whole place, she felt, looked different, but she wasn't sure why or how. The furniture, apart from one bureau, was that supplied with the flat, mostly built-in, but apart from that, where Molly had always kept the place bright with flowers from spring onwards until late autumn, and then with bulbs or flowering pot plants, now there was nothing but a stark simplicity which looked, she thought, surprised at her own mental picture, something like a modern counterpart of the cell of a monk in days of long ago.

Whatever there had been of Ann's which might have made the flat into an individual home was gone.

'It'll all be packed in one or other of those cases, boxes and bags she had,' Elizabeth decided, and then wondered, ridiculously, what else had been packed in the small trunk which had gone away in the back of the taxi.

It really didn't matter, she decided. It certainly couldn't have been anything as dramatic as a body, for the only other occupant of the flat was standing beside her, issuing instructions as she took from a large black medical man's case the syringe and a small bottle of fluid from which he carefully measured out two drops into the small, now sterilised bowl he had taken from somewhere in one of the two bedrooms.

'Clean towels in that drawer,' he directed, 'and now if you'll incline his head . . .'

Roger's crying had dwindled away to a few irregular sobs, and as Elizabeth held him firmly, head over the bowl, she felt the tension in the small body and then the gradual relaxation as he found out this was not, after all, to be a painful matter.

Elizabeth had seen Michael at work on the wards, but this was the first time she had seen him in actuality exactly as she had so often pictured him. This was the man who, she felt, would make the perfect general practitioner. His manner inspired confidence in his patient, and, as she watched and anticipated his every move, Elizabeth felt something of the tension she had scarcely been aware of dropping from her own limbs also.

The same thought must have occurred to Michael, for suddenly, after syringing for the second time, he turned his head deliberately and smiled at her.

'Don't look so worried, Elizabeth,' he advised. 'I once performed an emergency tracheotomy with nothing more available than a very nervous mother, a kitchen table and a pillow and—all I had with me at the time, since I was on a walking holiday—a small, very sharp penknife which I sterilised and with which I worked.' She said nothing for a moment, and his smile deepened. 'The patient lived,' he added, and was rewarded by her answering smile.

It took three times before the small drowned body of the little insect floated to the surface of the bowl. Michael and Elizabeth looked at it in relief. Roger with angry pleasure.

'Dat's it!' he pointed excitedly with one grubby finger. 'Dat's the nasty beetle that made Roger's ear hurt . . . dere!' and before either of them was aware of what he intended to do, he had tipped the bowl over, beetle, water and all, on to the carpet.

'Dat's got rid of him!' he said with satisfaction, and as Elizabeth sought for a cloth to clean up the mess she smiled to hear Michael quietly reproving the child.

Roger stared at him in amazement, then asked with a childlike innocence which was totally devoid of any

intended sarcasm: 'Ain't you goin' to 'it me, then? An'
look what a mess I made!'

Michael picked him up again, still talking quietly and
still explaining that Roger's action had not hurt the
beetle, it was already dead. But his action had made a lot
of work for Nurse, 'And it really isn't anything like the
sort of work she usually does!' he was saying as he
carried the child back to his mother.

Elizabeth smiled. What effect Michael's words would
have on the child, if indeed they had any at all, she could
not imagine. His life was an alternation of kisses and
blows, and there was small wonder he had difficulty in
getting his sense of values into proper focus. Small
wonder either that little Miss Lister, in her own failing
state of health, had not thought to inspect the child when
she had rejoined him on the grass.

'Though I doubt if many modern mothers would think
of doing so either, unless they'd read of or seen something like this happen,' she reflected.

She made the place as tidy as it had been when they
had entered, lingering for a moment and chiding herself
mentally for doing so, as she tried to picture Michael
here alone, night after night, writing his notes—he had
told her he was working on a book—or reading. She
shook herself free of dreams. That way lay nowhere.
Dreams were something which didn't belong to this
harsh world of reality, where a man like Michael Lloyd
could be deserted for someone who had a devil-may-
care air, and a way with the ladies.

She went quietly downstairs as she heard his voice
raised a little this time, and using the authoritative tone
she had heard him use only on the ward and then only
under extreme conditions.

Mrs Forrest, little Roger clutched once more firmly to her ample bust, was standing facing Michael as though about to challenge him. Over in the far corner of the room Miss Lister stood, twisting a scrap of linen and lace which had once been a fancy handkerchief, between her fingers. The spinster's face was ravaged by tears and relief, and Elizabeth, who crossed the room to her at once, was horrified to discover she was still shaking from head to foot as though with an ague.

'And,' Michael's voice continued inexorable as he addressed the now silent Mrs Forrest, 'as you have just told me you are almost twenty-eight years of age and I happen to know Miss Lister is almost eighty-two, just the figures in reverse, isn't it? Don't you think it would be far better if you took the children to the playground yourself every afternoon. instead of doing whatever it is you do to amuse yourself? I understand you don't go to work . . .'

'We've no need of that, Doctor, thank you!' Mrs Forrest's spirit was by no means quelled, but she did not sound one half so sure of herself as she had done a few minutes ago. .

'Then you should be thankful,' Michael said sternly. The little you tell me you have the effrontery to offer Miss Lister for her care three afternoons of each week wouldn't keep her two cats and the bird in food, and I am perfectly certain the children are far more of a worry to her than her pets have ever been or are likely to be.'

'I didn't think I was doing any harm,' Mrs Forrest said sullenly. 'I thought the few quid a week would be a help, and I don't miss it, not half so much as I'll miss my afternoon games with the others.'

'Then I'd advise you to find a game in which the

children can take a part, or pay for them to join a
registered play-group or nursery, as soon as possible,'
Michael said sternly, then, with a smile at Miss Lister
he opened the door wide and ushered the woman out.

Elizabeth had settled the old lady down in her
favourite chair, one of her cats on her knee, the other
arching his back and purring round her legs as though he
wanted to assure himself that all was now well with his
beloved mistress. Miss Lister herself had stopped twisting her hands and crying, but she was still trembling as
Elizabeth sought to restore her sense of proportion.

It took a great deal of gentle persuasion to convince
the old lady she had not been to blame, most people,
Elizabeth assured her, would have done precisely the
same thing, by attempting to poke out the offending
intruder with the pointed end of a clean handkerchief.

'It's quite a frequent mistake,' Elizabeth said yet
again. 'Just as it is when a child pokes something up his
or her nose or swallows a foreign body. It's far better to
go at once to the casualty department of the nearest
hospital, or to any First Aid Post—and there is one in the
park, I think—and let someone who's been trained in
these matters take complete charge. It's better for the
child, and far less wearing on the nerves of whoever was
in charge of the kiddies at the time. You'll remember
another time, won't you?' she coaxed.

'You needn't worry, Nurse,' the old lady gulped.
'There won't be another time. I thought it was two
pounds easily earned—I like looking after them, you
see, and I like to see the ducks and walk in the park
myself, and the children were company—but not any
more.'

'Would you mind if I had a word with our Social

Worker about you, Miss Lister?' Elizabeth felt she had a flash of inspiration. 'She's a wonderful person, and she'll be able to help. There's a Senior Citizens' Group she's in touch with. You could find someone there, no doubt, with whom you could have your walks and talks without responsibility of this nature. And if the two pounds is of such great importance . . .' she hesitated a moment, knowing how sensitive was Miss Lister's pride, 'then I'm sure she'll be able to help you arrange what you have to pay out so that you can manage without having to do this sort of thing to help make ends meet.'

She was thinking along the lines of help in paying the old lady's rent or her fuel and light bills, and to her surprised relief Miss Lister appeared to have accepted the suggestion without a fight.

'Thank you, Nurse,' she said, in the tone of one who is giving an approving pat on the head to a child. 'You have been more than helpful, and I am very grateful. I should like to know about these Senior Citizens. I don't see any reason why I can't qualify for that!'

There was a world of bitterness in her voice, and as she and Michael left the room and went slowly back upstairs, Elizabeth was abruptly hit by the feeling of how useless someone like Miss Lister must feel when faced with a crisis of this nature. A mental picture of her own grandmother, secure in the love of a large family, flashed before her eyes, and before she knew what was happening she felt tears form and spill over, a kind of mute protest at the unfairness of life in general.

'Here!' They were inside her own flat now and Michael was eyeing her with genuine concern. 'Take this,' he advised, holding out a huge clean handkerchief, 'and have a good blow!'

Elizabeth did as she was told when all at once every sense leapt into action as Michael put a casual arm about her shoulders, drawing her closer to him. That seemed to be the final straw. With a shuddering sigh she let herself relax against his chest and the tears poured unchecked down her cheeks.

CHAPTER EIGHT

IF Michael was as surprised by this sudden outburst of emotion as was Elizabeth herself, he betrayed nothing of the fact. He patted her shoulder comfortingly, making soothing sounds which might or might not have been interpreted as anything personal. He appeared to find nothing unusual in this state of nerves, but Elizabeth, after the first moment or so's emotion had spent itself, felt suddenly and completely ashamed.

'I'm sorry,' she said, sniffing in a most unladylike manner. 'I've no idea why I've behaved in that idiotic fashion.'

'Haven't you, Elizabeth?' Michael asked softly. 'I think you have. You've learned a great deal about emotions and emotional situations in the course of your work, and for some reason or another you were completely strung up, nervewise, before all this happened. I could sense it the moment I asked you about some milk.'

In that case, her thoughts ran on undisciplined, why couldn't he realise that her concern, her nerves being what he termed 'strung up', had been on his account and not on her own? Why couldn't he realise that seeing Ann and Dr Bickersley drive off together had made her so thoroughly unhappy for the remainder of the day that she could think of little else but of Michael's own disappointment and distress when he returned to the flat?

When he had returned he had seemed happier than

she had ever seen him, and to crown everything he had admitted he had known Ann and Roland were going away . . . and that he would be seeing them tomorrow.

'To arrange about the divorce, I suppose,' she said, and did not realise she had spoken the words aloud until Michael took a shocked hand from her shoulders and held her at arms' length, scrutinising her closely.

'Divorce?' he repeated. 'Whose divorce? You've not been hiding a secret husband from me all the time I've known you, have you, Elizabeth?'

'Not my divorce,' she managed at length. 'Yours.'

It was Michael's turn to stare in astonishment, and, then, quite abruptly, he began to laugh, laughter which was instantly stilled as he saw her ashen face.

'My poor little sweet,' he said with a tenderness she had never heard him use before, not even with a very sick patient, 'what *have* you been imagining? And all the time, both Ann and I expected everyone here would know her story and have their own versions of it, just as Roland had. He'd only read about it in the papers, of course, but he's been through something of the same kind himself, some years ago, and he knew what it was like—all the publicity, the enquiries and all the talk.'

'I don't understand,' Elizabeth said flatly, sitting down in one of the armchairs because without the support of his arm she had the strangest feeling that her legs would fail to support her.

'It's very simple, really,' Michael perched himself on the arm of the chair, not touching her, but so close she could hear the beating of his heart.

'Ann's not my wife,' he explained, and then, as she still looked as though she couldn't accept that as a fact, he went on to explain patiently. 'She was married to my twin brother, Robert,' he said firmly. 'I told you about Bobby, remember? That was the name everyone knew him by, even the newspapers had got hold of it, and I thought you knew.'

'I thought she was *your* wife.' Elizabeth felt she must sound as stupid as she felt, but Michael evidently did not think so.

'No,' he repeated. 'Bobby and I were very much alike in some things, but our personalities were almost directly opposite. That was why I felt if anyone had to look after Ann until she found her bearings again, it would have to be myself.'

'Something happened to . . . Bobby?'

'Remember the bush fires in Australia some time ago?' Michael asked, and as she nodded he continued. 'They were working together on a research station, something to do with the sort of bugs we might expect to collect if people go on landing on other planets and bringing what Ann terms "alien dust", back here. They had to work in the bush because most of the plants they were working with grow there, and it so happened when the fires started, they were so absorbed in what they were doing they almost left it too late for anything . . . or anyone . . . to be salvaged.'

'Bobby . . . died?' It was a statement rather than a question. Michael nodded.

'According to Ann he needn't have died, either,' he said, suddenly very quiet and grave. 'There was a young boy who helped them by gathering the particular plant-life they required. They were both extremely fond of him. He'd been orphaned almost all his life, and I think they both looked upon him as part of the family they hadn't had time to have for themselves.'

'And?' Elizabeth probed, as he paused.

'When the fires started they tried to get as much equipment—and as many results of their experiments as they could—safely away, naturally. It seems this boy ran back and forth, bringing one load after another to put in the jeep. Ann was stacking things inside and outside, trying to make the most of every possible inch of space; Bobby and the boy were dashing in and out, trying to beat the flames.'

He was silent for so long she thought he had lost the thread of his story, but all at once he began to speak again.

'Ann says she remembers Tommy—that was what they called the boy because it was easier to say than the name he'd been given when he was born—running back because there was something, I don't know what it was, he felt was sufficiently important to Bobby to be saved at all costs. Naturally Bobby had told him to leave it—the flames, it seems, spread like wildfire, which isn't surprising when you think of the dryness of the timber and of the number of eucalyptus trees there are! Tommy ignored the order, and rushed off back to what had been their work-shed, Bobby pounding after him. That was the last she saw of them for a long time, and then it was only a badly burned Tommy she saw. They didn't find . . . what was left of Bobby. His bones and bits would be so much ash by then, I suppose.'

'Poor Ann!' Elizabeth's voice was gentle with sympathy. She could well understand the reason for the look of the lone Madonna, the playing and replaying of the two mournful records which had so unnerved everyone when the Lloyds had first come to Landawne House.

'You'd have felt even more sorry for her if you'd seen

her when I went to bring her home,' Michael said gently, his voice soft with the memory. 'She was almost in a state of collapse. She and Bobby adored one another, and they had worked together for so many years and on so many schemes like this one. It took me all of a month to persuade her that Tommy would be well enough looked after in the home we found, where he'll be taught a useful trade and where, in time, he'll regain his self-confidence. Somehow that seemed to have been burned away along with a lot of other things . . . Bobby included.'

'They had no family?' Elizabeth persisted. She knew she was in all probability probing a sore wound, but somehow she felt now she had to know as much of Ann as was possible. At least she could apologise by proxy if her visit, when she had first tried to be just friendly, had seemed to Ann like a further show of the vulgar curiosity she must have grown to expect.

'They had one child, a boy,' Michael said. 'He didn't live more than a few hours, something wrong with his bloodstream. That was what gave Bobby the idea of investigating all he could about what was finally going to happen to this old earth when we've all finished throwing missiles into the sky, treading alien soil and all the rest of it. Ann was behind him all the way. They made a grand team, but it upset Dad and Mother a great deal, because they seemed to want never to come back home again.' He paused. 'Perhaps that was because of the child,' he said quietly. 'I should imagine a thing like that could produce just such an effect.'

'I should imagine so,' Elizabeth agreed. 'I wish I'd known.'

'Then you wouldn't have held me at arm's length all

this time and treated me as though I was just another doctor, come to Jude's on a short-term basis, would you?' Michael joked, but before she could reply the door opened and Joan rushed in, headlong, as usual.

'Oh!' Her exclamation, for some unknown reason, struck Elizabeth as being ludicrous, and she had the greatest difficulty in repressing a fit of giggles.

This was dreadful, she thought, angry with herself. First she had wept all over Michael, and just when she thought she was so sorry for him, and really it must have been because she was sorry for herself. Now, perhaps because of the relief, she wanted to laugh, and she could well imagine Joan's face if the usually very self-controlled Elizabeth were to suddenly burst into what would seem like uncalled for and uncontrolled mirth, as she remembered a lecturer reproving her class once, in her PTS days.

'It's all right,' she began in what she hoped was a normal tone of voice. 'We've just had a hoo-hah with Mrs Forrest and one of her infants, involving poor little Miss Lister, but it's all over now, thank goodness.'

'Pardon me,' Michael's eyes twinkled mischievously as Elizabeth could see by his reflection in the mirror, 'but it's by no means all over now. On the contrary, it's just beginning! Nurse Barstow, do you know of a good wine shop anywhere close by where we might find a good quality champagne? I rather think we shall have something to celebrate in a little while—or at any rate I *hope* we shall!'

'There's Sheppertons', on the corner of the precinct,' Joan said, hesitating. 'But they're awfully expensive . . . maybe . . .'

'I should imagine there'll be enough here, wouldn't

you?' Michael pulled some notes from his wallet and handed them to Joan without even counting them. 'And bring Tim along with you, will you?' he called after her retreating form.

When the door had closed quietly behind the suddenly enthusiastic Joan, he turned deliberately and put his arms fully about the girl in the chair.

'Won't you stand up, darling?' he said gently. 'I can't put my arms about you without taking in the chair as well . . . or would you rather I didn't . . . ?'

'Oh, Michael!' was all the inadequate answer Elizabeth could find at that moment, but it appeared to be more than enough. His arms tightened about her as he slowly drew her to her feet.

'It's not a conventional way of proposing, I know,' he said with a grin, 'but will you marry me, Elizabeth? I've loved you ever since the day you asked me back in here when I'd been down to see Bill. If I hadn't known, when I first met you at Jude's you were just the sort of girl I've waited all my life to find, what Joan had said first, and then what Bill told me—and everyone else on the staff of the hospital or in Landawne House—would have had me convinced right away. Give in your notice, darling, by all means. Yes, I heard you'd contemplated doing exactly that, though I don't know why. Then come to Boldearne. There hasn't been a nurse as the Doctor's wife since Mother had to give it up, some years ago. Will you do that?'

What Elizabeth said in reply was never recorded, but when an over-exuberant Joan returned some minutes later accompanied by a beaming Tim clutching two bottles of the best champagne the store could offer, she had almost, but not quite, recovered her composure.

'We'll drink to us,' Michael announced, 'to the four of us. What about a double wedding—before the end of the month, then Ann and Roland can attend?'

There were discussions and plans to be made. Joan had not expected to be married until the end of the year, but Tim pooh-poohed that idea by saying he could get an advance from his bank now he had finally got fixed up with a small partnership in the group practice.

Elizabeth had always dreamed of a quiet wedding in the little old village church at home, with all the old friends of her schooldays members of the congregation.

At Joan's prompting she counted up who was left of those with whom she had gone to school, and the number was so surprisingly small she was more than willing to agree to Michael's suggestion that the double wedding be held in St Mary's, Malenchester, where all their friends from Jude's (those who were not on duty) could attend.

'It'll be a trip out, down south or up north, depending on direction, for the relatives,' he joked. 'Ann and Roland are flying to the Far East at the beginning of next month. They'll be staying with Mother and Dad for a week or so, and it would be wonderful if we could go up then and see the folks, introduce you around the place as the new doctor's wife . . . and the nurse-receptionist. I warn you, old Nurse Bateson has been our District for more years than I care to remember. She must be nearly due to retire, but she'll go a great deal more happy than if she'd left what she always refers to as "the care of my folks" to just one young girl, fresh on District, and no nurse at the Doctor's to help out. What do you say, love?'

'I don't appear to have much option!' Elizabeth

THE PURSUIT OF DR LLOYD

laughed, and with sparkling eyes she raised her glass in company with the others as Michael proposed 'The Four of Us', and they all drank.

Doctor Nurse Romances

Romance in the wide world of medicine

Amongst the intense emotional pressures of modern medical life, doctors and nurses often find romance. Read about their lives and loves in the other two Doctor Nurse titles available this month.

DOCTOR HARTNELL'S DISCOVERY
by Elizabeth Petty

While out riding, Sister Lara Groves rescues a man who has been badly injured in a fall from his horse. But when he turns out to be the new consultant at the hospital where she works, it seems that that chance meeting will lead to nothing but heartache.

TALISMAN FOR A SURGEON
by Lisa Cooper

Sister Rosalind Mason feels upset and humiliated after her rows with the suave, elegant and eminent surgeon, Peregrine Bradford. But as a friend warns her, hatred is akin to love . . .

Mills & Boon
the rose of romance